Molly's Missing

ISBN: 978-0-9955640-0-8

First Edition November 2016
Higher Visions Publishing
Marymead, Cholsey, Oxfordshire

Printed in the UK for Higher Visions Publishing by
Catford Printing Centre, Catford, London

Molly's Missing

From the Vicki and Dennis Series

by
John R. Fyfe

Illustrations © by Linda C. Graham

This book is dedicated to
Dennis Pratt

Acknowledgments

Many thanks go to

Atula for her wonderful contributions

And
Linda Graham for her fine artwork and
her patient help with the completion of this book

INDEX

CHAPTER 1   5-22
CHAPTER 2   23-29
CHAPTER 3   30-34
CHAPTER 4   35-42
CHAPTER 5   43-57
CHAPTER 6   58-70
CHAPTER 7   71-89

ILLUSTRATIONS
Vicki and Dennis   6
Rabbits flats, Duncan, Maisy and Daisy   9
Molly and Bounder   12
Down by the rock pond   18
The big beech tree   19
Breakfast at the Pratt's house   26
Molly escapes from the electrical van   38
Duncan relayed the message from the Angels to the   42
Faeries
Molly sat like a bird on a branch hidden and content.   46
Father Jim with pretty boy on his head   49
Dennis finds the watch and shoes   63
Dennis helps with the cage   72
Molly is dropped into the blanket   82
Molly being hugged by Vicky   86

CHAPTER ONE

Summary Morning

It was 6:45 a.m. in the Pratt house, and already the bright morning sun shone its rays into the upstairs bedroom where Vicky and Dennis slept. Through the open window, chirping sounds could be heard as mother birds fed their babies fresh worms scooped from the earth, damp from the morning dew.

Dennis was the first to wake, and rubbing the corners of his eyes he said, rather loudly and not at all concerned that Vicky was still asleep, "The sandman came again last night."

He jumped out of bed and called to his sister, where she was curled beneath the blankets with her cat Molly lying on top of her legs, purring contently. Dennis shouted to both of them, "Wake up sleepyheads!"

Molly stretched, arching her slinky body the way cats often do. Vicky, upon waking, opened her large blue eyes and, realizing what day it was, yelled with excitement.

"Yippee! Summer holidays are here!" Kissing the top of her tabby's head she then said, "That means no school for me, Molly dear!"

You see, Molly was Vicky's cat and Bounder belonged to Dennis.

Bounder was the protector of the house. He was a warrior (the peaceful kind), who always made sure the territory outside the family's home was safe from other cats getting too close, as well as any other animals looking for trouble. He'd been up since the crack of dawn, before anyone else, and had jumped

5

from the open bedroom window onto the tree branch outside to climb down the large beech tree. He had serious business to attend to being an explorer and all.

Molly, however, had more of a gentle nature. She was no warrior, instead loving to investigate hidden nooks and crannies; often Vicky saw her emerge from a hole in the fence, with specks of dust hanging from her whiskers, or peeking out from behind boxes in the garage. Molly couldn't help herself from browsing around these hidden areas early in the morning, but today, with Vicky home, still in bed, she enjoyed sleeping on her legs, knowing this was the very best place to be.

Pulling his bright t-shirt over his short brown hair, Dennis again shouted to his sister, saying, "Come on, Vicky! Get out bed! Let's go see Bounder and the rabbits out by the shed."

His dark blue eyes glowed with excitement, thinking about all the plans he had for that day. Today was going to be an adventure. It was the beginning of summer holidays!

Vicky and Dennis

Dennis was a little skinny, but that's because he was tall for his age. His sister always warned him never to be outside on a windy day, where he might be blown away and they'd never see him again! This made Dennis a little worried when it came to windy days, but he knew he was stronger than Vicky thought; because he was a boy, and boys grew stronger and bigger everyday. Vicky had dark blonde hair often tied into pigtails, with bright blue eyes the colour of the sky on a sunny, cloudless day. Her face was perfectly round and full of freckles, which she was told would fade as she got older. Her brother loved calling her freckly-face for this made her mad; little did he know that

6

sometimes, it also made her sad.

"Come on Vicky, the rabbits want to be fed," Dennis said, as he found his shoes under his bed.

After pulling on their clothes, Vicky and Dennis rushed down the narrow hallway with Molly leading the way. They passed their mother and father's bedroom door - they were still fast asleep.

"Ssshh!" Vicky whispered to her brother as he stomped down the stairs. "Don't make so much noise! You sound just like all the other boys!"

Dennis pushed past, sticking his tongue out at her. Vicky shook her head, thinking what a child her brother was, for she was nine years-old and much more mature than her brother, who was seven.

Meeting with the rabbits

Vicky and Dennis opened the backdoor, and went running into the yard. The grass was quite long, with weeds growing here and there, and the hedges were overgrown. The children's father, whose name was Jim, was always forgetting to tend the garden. Jim, or James as Mother Pratt sometimes called him when she needed him to pay attention to household chores, was always thinking about different projects and ideas while working on his computer. He was often scribbling on pieces of paper which he'd stash in the back pocket. Days would go by before he once again remembered about the garden chores.

"Oh, dear!" Father Jim would exclaim, slapping his hand to his forehead. "I forgot to mow the lawn again." Then he would sigh, and ask himself, "Wherever does the time go? Well, I must remember to absolutely do it tomorrow."

Father Jim was always saying time just flew by, and Dennis, hearing his father say this, imagined the hands of a clock speeding 'round and 'round. It was something even adults couldn't change, as nobody is able to slow down time. Then another day arrived and Father Jim would return from work, say hello to everyone - even the cats - and go write on his computer. After dinner he would watch the telly, once again forgetting all about the grass and the hedges.

Vicky and Dennis enjoyed their father's forgetfulness; since he was always working something out in his head, they thought he was a brilliant thinker. However, people who didn't know him so well, thought he was eccentric, a polite word people used instead of calling him strange.

So it was, as Vicky and Dennis arrived slightly breathless at the rabbit's hutch where Maisy, Daisy and Duncan lived.

Bounder was lying comfortably on top of the hutches, taking in the sun's warm rays after having a busy morning and as we all know, cats love to sit and nap whenever they have a chance to do so.

Bounder and Molly were not like most other cats who would try to bite or scratch the rabbits. They played with Maisy, Daisy and Duncan whenever Vicky and Dennis took them out of their hutches, as they were doing at this very moment.

"I think you should feed them first," Vicky suggested to Dennis. "Or give them some water to quench their thirst."

Dennis made a sour face at his sister. "You worry far too much," he said, while opening the cages. "And I don't know what that word quench means."

"It means to satisfy your thirst, dummy!" Vicky said in a know-it-all-voice. "How many times have you heard that word used by Mummy?"

Dennis gently pulled at Vicky's pigtails, laughing off his sister's insult. Although, at times they teased each other, Vicky and Dennis rarely fought for they loved each other so much. Dennis laughed again while watching Bounder and Molly imitate the rabbits, as they hip-hopped over the long, uncut grass. "Look!" He said. "The cats are trying to be rabbits!"

"Or is it because they both know each others' habits?" Vicky replied.

When the rabbits stopped jumping so did Bounder and Molly, as they seemed to be copying the rabbits' movement, much to the delight of the children, who watched wide-eyed. Vicky joined in with her furry friends, rolling on the grass beside Maisy, Daisy and Duncan. Bounder and Molly, finished with their play, stretched out beside her.

"I could stay in this garden forever," Vicky said to Dennis. "I'd live with the rabbits and cats, and sing with the birds and fly with the bats!"

"Yech!" Dennis screwed up his face in disgust, not quite understanding why his sister would want to do such a thing with bats. "I wouldn't want to fly with the bats," he exclaimed. "But I could live with the rabbits and play with the cats."

Dennis joined his sister, sprawling on the grass beside the rabbits and stroking Maisy's soft, fluffy white fur.

Maisy and Daisy were sisters, with identical white coats. They were almost three years-old, according to Vicky, who had the best memory of all and therefore took after her mother, not Father Jim. The hutches had three levels, like a small apartment building; one for Duncan, one for Maisy and another for Daisy. But Maisy and Daisy liked sleeping together, so often one of their apartments was empty, at least during the night.

Rabbits flats, Duncan, Maisy and Daisy

9

Maisy was expecting babies any day now, and everyone in the house, including Mother Pratt and Father Jim, were quite excited, all wondering how many baby rabbits there would be. Duncan, who lived in his own hutch upstairs from Maisy and Daisy, was also excited with the unexpected arrival, *(at least as much as a rabbit can be)* for he was the father.

Duncan had golden, light-brown fur and was a serious rabbit, much more so than Maisy and Daisy. When in such moods, Duncan looked like he was sulking, but he was only thinking, for Duncan was a very wise rabbit, much wiser than people could ever imagine.

The most wonderful thing was that Maisy, Daisy and Duncan could speak to each other, but Duncan could also speak to other animals as well, including Bounder and Molly. However, they didn't speak as people did, but communicated with each other, through their thoughts.

"If only Dennis and Vicky knew that we can talk to each other," Duncan said through his thoughts to Maisy, twitching his nose at her

Maisy agreed, twitching her nose in response, for she knew that Duncan was wise, being the oldest at five years-old, and what he had to say was often important.

Bounder and Molly also knew that Duncan was wise, and the two of them would listen to his thoughts, sitting beneath the rabbit hutch or on the roof with eyes closed as if asleep. But they weren't asleep at all. They were listening to Duncan and the many stories that came from him.

****

As this was the first day of summer holidays, Molly was especially excited to have her best friend home from school. She felt lonely when Vicky was away, for Molly had the special ability to hear the thoughts of humans, especially Vicky's. Molly felt so connected to Vicky that she always wanted to be around her. Even if Molly was not sitting right beside her, she was content knowing that Vicky's presence was nearby. This is what energy is and Molly was very much in touch with Vicky's energy.

So, you could say that Molly was connected to Vicky, and Vicky was connected to Molly.

Vicky knew the energy of cats, knowing that they were most curious animals. They couldn't resist squeezing through the cracks of a fence, peeking around corners to investigate, or slipping through partially open doors.

Molly was so curious that she couldn't stop herself from snooping in the old garage at the back of their garden, or around the open garages of their neighbours, sometimes suddenly finding the garage doors shut by someone who didn't know she was inside. Molly would be locked in for short periods, but there were other times when she was locked in longer. It all depended on whether Vicky was home or not. When Vicky was home, she'd suddenly feel a missing energy connected to Molly, and immediately she knew something wasn't right and would go look for her. Sometimes she would hear a quiet meowing, and then try to figure out where the crying was coming from.

Often - much too often - thought Vicky, she would hear Molly crying from inside a garage or atop a big tree, unable to get down, for most cats cannot climb backwards. And as dangerous as it looked, Vicky would climb up and rescue her cat once again.

Molly's fur was a mixture of deep browns and greys, with black stripes on her back, a bit like a raccoon. She had a beautiful patch of fluffy white fur under her chin and on her belly, giving her a majestic appearance. She was a proud tabby cat much loved by her human family, as well as her animal family.

Bounder was slightly bigger than Molly, orange with white patches of fur under his chin which spread along to his belly just like Molly's. Although Bounder was extremely smart (as Bounder himself indeed thought), he knew Molly and Duncan were special because of their ability to hear the thoughts of people. At times, Bounder heard Dennis's thoughts, but not as easily as Molly could.

Bounder was Molly's protector. Sometimes the mean cats in town came close to the back garden and when seeing Molly on the other side of the fence, they'd try to pick a fight with her or claw her for no reason. Cat screams sometimes echoed across the yard and Bounder, not a fighter by nature, would rush out to defend Molly, knowing he was his sister's keeper so that no harm came her way.

Bounder also kept careful watch over the rabbits when they were out of their hutch, in case any stray animal ventured too close. Bounder was indeed the guardian, and he took pride in this role, doing it well because there much to protect... as we shall see.

Molly   and   Bounder

Meetings with the Angels & Faeries

Maisy and Daisy had special abilities as well because along with Duncan, they could see the Angels and Faeries fluttering about in the air, dashing through the tree branches and dancing in the shadows.

The Angels and Faeries are indeed everywhere! The Faeries delighted in passing wisdom to Duncan, who in return was pleased to be of service to them.

All animals feel the presence of the Angels and Faeries, as most everyone does really, except for human adults.

Grown-ups or Grumps, as the Faeries liked to call them, were far too busy to notice these things. Younger children, on the other hand, could either see the Angels and Faeries or at least feel their energies.

Human babies are always able to see the Angels floating around them as well as hear the beautiful angelic music being played. It is why human babies always seem to be staring into blank space much like cats do, but it's the Angels they are seeing, not empty space.

"Just because you cannot see things doesn't mean they are not there," the Faeries would tell Duncan as he lay snug as a bug in his hutch at nighttime.

Human children are so often told by adults that they are only dreaming when they mention that they see the Angels and Faeries.

"Don't be silly dear," is a favourite expression of adults, who have sadly lost touch with the Faerie world. Another common statement is, "It's only your imagination running away with you."

When children begin to get older, they start to doubt the existence of Angels and Faeries because they have been told so many times by the adults that they are being foolish. The Angels and Faeries then disappear from their sight, but no matter what, they are still there.

****

Dennis and Vicky felt energy in many ways, but were not able to see the Angels and Faeries anymore, although somewhere inside they still believed in them. The adult world was already beginning to affect them.

Every human adult was of course at one time a tiny baby and the Angels and Faeries were always a part of their life back then, but as they became older they started to forget, until there was no more remembering and that, sadly, is what happens with adults. But that doesn't have to happen! Not if you believe!

Every day when Maisy, Daisy and Duncan, were jumping about in the yard, they saw little bright specks of light flickering about and they knew that these bright specks were the Angels. At night, their white light became easier to see, glowing in the garden by the rabbit hutch much like fireflies. In fact, the fireflies were the Faeries, and the Angels were the tiny balls of light.

These balls of Angel light were harder to see because they didn't glitter like the fireflies, but the Angels were certainly inside these little balls of light and if you squeezed your eyes hard enough, squinting, you could see the tiny white Angels fluttering about in them. And on special evenings, when the wind was silent and the leaves on the branches were still, the Angels and Faeries would float about the rabbit hutch speaking in Faerie tongue to Maisy, Daisy and especially Duncan. For Duncan took their words in much more seriously than did the other two rabbits, who usually drifted off to sleep upon listening to the musical voices of the Faeries. It was like a sweet lullaby being sung to them.

Duncan enjoyed the singing as well, but being serious, he was more interested in hearing what the Angels had to say, so he concentrated really hard not to fall asleep.

The Angels know everything about the world. They know

that the world is full of spirit with feelings and thoughts which are much different from how the human adult world thinks.

The Angels told Duncan that the trees could indeed speak to each other, especially during windy days because the branches swaying in the wind were bending closer to one another, making it easier for them to hear.

The Angels told Duncan, "Flowers and grass also have energy, as well as the insects like bumble bees, who know by instinct to take in the energy of nectar from the flowers to make honey. Even the rocks are alive because there is energy inside rocks. We are all energy Duncan." The Angels would spread out their wings and repeat, "All of us! All of us!"

Duncan stayed up most nights listening to the Angels speak of love, as they would explain how most human adults and even some children forgot about love, or why they refused to feel love. "It all comes down to belief, Duncan, belief. We must believe that love exists, and that Angels and Faeries exist. And we mustn't forget about the elves, Duncan, for the elves are part of the Faerie world, as are the dwarfs and gnomes."

The Angels continued, "You see Duncan, We Angels look after everyone in this world. We are the guides for everything that exists. The Faeries look after all the plants, the trees and the rocks. And the Sidhe (pronounced Shee) are the invisible people who look after the Faeries, advising them on what to do with the plants."

In Duncan's head, their voices sounded like a violin gently playing, and he felt tempted to take just a little nap. He watched the Angels and the Faeries float around the garden, their words sounding like a choir playing a beautiful song. Duncan knew this was available for all humans, if only they allowed themselves the chance to listen. If only, he thought sadly, if only.

****

The Angels had told Duncan just last night that it was high time for people to slow down their busy lives, so they could hear all the things that every animal and plant hears. They told Duncan that children are far more open than the adults. Children only had to ask the Angels and Faeries to come to them, for by doing so, the children were saying that they believed in them.

"When the children don't ask for us, Duncan," said a firefly that was a Faerie, whose voice sent tingles up his spine. "We're not allowed to come because they won't hear us. They must first believe in us, at least a little bit. If they can open up their hearts to that, then that is good enough." The Faerie who was a firefly floated lightly across Duncan's furry back and continued to speak.

"The children don't really have to speak to us, for we know what they think and feel without needing words... and no matter, the Angels will watch over them, whether they believe in us or not."

Duncan had many more questions to ask the Angels, especially one that he was most curious about. "Did I ask to see the Angels at the beginning of my life? And did Maisy and Daisy ask, as well as Bounder and Molly?"

A pixie Angel with beautiful pink wings had been quietly watching from afar while Duncan twitched his rabbit nose and chewed his fresh lettuce, spoke. "Yes, Duncan," she whispered. "You asked for us right from the beginning. Although animals are different. They don't think the same way as humans with all their questions and doubts. Animals know right from the beginning and continue knowing."

A sudden gust of wind came and the Faeries went topsy-turvy in the crisp night air, letting out a chorus of giggling laughter, as everything in the world gave them joy and love.

"Human babies know from the beginning, Duncan, but when they become young children, too many thoughts and activities begin to take over, and little by little they forget about

16

us, but not completely. There is still a tiny piece of us left inside, which has only fallen asleep and can be awakened at anytime simply by believing in us."

That was a lot of information for Duncan to remember, so he bid the Angels and Faeries good-night as he lay in his comfortable, warm straw bed, and fell into a deep, blissful sleep, still dreaming of them.

Down by the rock-pond

The sun was beginning to climb above the trees and the human world was waking up. The clanging of dishes could be heard from the Pratt's kitchen, as well as from the houses of their neighbours and tea kettles whistled, blowing off their steam.

The white tips of Maisy, Daisy and Duncan's fluffy tails were visible as they hopped through the long grass.

"Let's visit the frogs in the pond," Duncan suggested. Maisy and Daisy were now huddled together, nibbling pieces of lettuce that Vicky had brought out for them. Duncan was gazing towards the pond, having already eaten enough of his lettuce.

Dennis and Vicky's father had lovingly built the rock-pond two years earlier. Father Jim had a great ability to create the most wonderful things when he applied his mind towards not forgetting! The children, who were still waiting for the breakfast call from their mother, went with the rabbits towards the pond, carefully walking around the prickly berry bushes to an open clearing, where the tiny pool was. They leaned, face-down on their tummies, looking over the edge of the rocks that surrounded the pond, and gazed into the stillness of the water. For it was a quiet day with only a slight breeze, not strong enough to create even a tiny ripple on the water's surface.

Bounder and Molly, who chose not to follow their friends, jumped onto the old wooden picnic table perfectly placed under the shade of the giant beech tree. That was the tree

Bounder climbed down from the bedroom window, as Bounder was different type of cat who wasn't afraid to climb down trees.

****

The frogs were making loud croaking noises, as they gobbled insects who dared to fly too close to them.

"How many frogs do you think are in the pond, Dennis?" Vicky asked her brother.

'Ten!' Duncan the rabbit answered in his mind, twitching his nose and sending his thoughts to Dennis.

"I don't know," Dennis said at first, looking into the pond. But then he suddenly said, "I would say ten."

"I like that guess," Vicky said, quite satisfied. "Because I have already counted ten, so you need not guess again!"

"How many frogs do you think are in the pond, Dennis?" Vicky asked her brother.

The three rabbits twitched their noses like they were sharing a joke, and of course they were. Vicky didn't know

Duncan gave the answer to Dennis and Dennis didn't know that he could hear Duncan's thoughts.

Molly said to Bounder in her purring voice as they lay on the table watching the proceedings, "It's good that Vicky and Dennis can hear us speak to them, even when they don't know it."

Bounder flicked his tail in agreement, watching Molly stretch out, showing off the white fur on her tummy.

The back garden where Vicky and Dennis played, was not overly large, although to them it seemed gigantic.

It was longer than it was wide and appeared bigger because of everything that was in it. There was the tool shed at the back of the garden with the little pond in the middle and the rabbit hutches were on one side of the fence where the hedges were. There were flowers and potted plants on the other side of the garden. All of this made the garden look full and large. Of course we mustn't forget about the big beech tree.

The beech tree

The back garden was truly the most favourite spot in the world for Vicky and Dennis.

A sudden gust of wind blew five very bright-green dragonflies over the rabbits' heads, and Dennis laughed in surprise as he jumped up and tried to catch them in his hands, but they escaped over the pond.

"Did you see the Faeries?" Duncan asked Maisy and Daisy, twitching his nose with a chuckle.

"Vicky and Dennis think they are only dragonflies."

"Yes!" cried Maisy.

"Yes indeed!" said Daisy, hearing Duncan's thoughts. "We see the Faeries, Duncan! We see the Faeries!"

A Dragonfly-Faerie circled around Dennis's head, while another landed on Vicky's shoulder. However, it remained there only for a few seconds, because Dennis reached out to catch him and Faeries cannot be touched by human hands, or they will disappear. The dragonfly Faerie didn't want to alarm Vicky and Dennis by vanishing before their very eyes.

Because the early morning sun was casting shadows, there were specks of light dancing everywhere around them, but only the animals could see this clearly, as Vicky and Dennis were far too busy with their thoughts and activities to notice.

Dennis kicked at a rock, trying to free it from the ground it was buried in. He wasn't concerned with the flashes of light around him. He was concentrating on the rock because he wanted to pry it out and throw it into the pond to watch the splash and hear the plop as it sank to the bottom.

The rabbits stomped their back paws on the ground as if they didn't agree with what Dennis was doing. He finally managed to dislodge the very old stone which was the size of a grapefruit and he chucked it into the pond. SPLASH! came the sound as the rock sank to the bottom, sending ripples of tiny waves around the pond.

The dragonflies once again flew around Dennis to distract him from looking for other rocks to throw and it worked. He began to chase them as they flew away from the pond and over towards the broken fence that Father Jim was supposed to fix, but had forgotten about, for now.

He stopped his chase when he saw a brilliant red and yellow butterfly flying towards him. It had so many beautiful colours on it, making him think of a rainbow. He watched it flutter past the pond headed towards the flowers.

Dennis thought it a miracle that this butterfly was once a wriggly old caterpillar climbing up tree branches, and now it was a beautiful rainbow-coloured creature with wings. He then thought about yesterday in the house when Vicky and Dennis's mother had noticed moths in the hallway cupboard. Mother Pratt had become quite upset finding those moths and was going to get her broom to kill them, because moths like to eat through clothes and everything else.

Vicky yelled in alarm when their mother came back with the broom to hit the moths. Vicky immediately began gathering them up in her hands. Dennis went over to help his sister and they each brought the moths one at a time to the downstairs window and very carefully (for moths are very fragile) released them to the outside world.

Mother Pratt didn't understand why Vicky wanted to save the moths.

Dennis wisely asked his mother, "What's the difference between a moth and a butterfly? You wouldn't kill a butterfly, would you?

"Because moths are trouble, Dennis," Mother said in a no nonsense voice. "They eat our clothes and lay their eggs on them, then they multiply. I just don't like moths!" she said sternly. "And if I see them in the house, I must kill them. There is no other choice."

Luckily for the moths, Vicky and Dennis were around to save them from such a fate.

Vicky had gone outside to sit by the pond with her rabbit friends, deep in thought, watching the ants with fascination as they worked on their anthill. Up and down they went, carrying pieces of dirt and wood that were much bigger than they were. She wondered how they knew where to go and how it was that they seemed to follow orders. Who gave them the instructions to march? And how strong they must be to do this work; the

21

ants were lifting more than twice the weight of their bodies! That would be like Vicky trying to carry a large bureau strapped on her shoulders as she walked down the street, quite an impossible task!

Next to the anthill was a spider's web and she saw a small, brown spider busily spinning its magic thread, weaving it further around the web, making it larger and stronger. The spider knew her web needed to be that strong and sticky to catch insects for food, so it was necessary to mend it often. Vicky wondered how the spider avoided getting stuck in her own web that she so wisely built to trap anything and everything that ventured too close.

Above Vicky, two young grey squirrels were chattering from the branches of the beech tree. They had been racing up and down the thick trunk chasing each other for sometime now, and it seemed that they were fighting-mad. It was then that the Dragonfly-Faeries floated up into the tree and sprinkled some Faerie dust around the squirrels, calming them down completely. They then started to play a game instead, as they climbed up the large beech tree. Their energy had changed.

The old beech tree was so tall that its branches stretched out high above the roof of their house, and in Dennis's eyes that was really high! Dennis thought he'd really like to climb the tree and jump onto the roof. "One day I will," he said to Bounder. "I want to stand on top of the world above the pond, the garden... the whole backyard!"

Dennis wondered if the beech tree went all the way to the sky, like in the story he had read about Jack and the beanstalk. 'Maybe,' he thought, "there was a giant that lived in the sky.

CHAPTER TWO

Breakfast at the Pratt house

Mother Pratt's name was Sue. She had curly brown hair that always seemed to get tangled after a night's sleep, so in the morning she always had a bit of a time brushing it out. While Vicky and Dennis were having their adventures in the back garden, Mother Pratt had been brushing her hair before preparing breakfast. When all of the activity was done, she opened the screen backdoor and called out to them.

"Vicky! Dennis! Come in now, breakfast is ready."

When Mother Pratt poked her head out the door to call them, the sparkling lights from the Angels immediately went dim, in case she got alarmed seeing the glow from the garden (if indeed Mother Pratt was ever able to see past her thoughts). For everyone can see the light emitted by the Angels, if they want to, as it's very, very easy... but the harder you try to see them, the more difficult it is. It has to be a natural thing, looking without looking, and that is very tricky for adults to do or to understand, but certainly not impossible.

Molly and Bounder, hearing Mother Pratt's voice, quickly jumped off the picnic table and ran through the open door into the kitchen, for they knew the breakfast call was also for them.

Vicky and Dennis followed the cats to the kitchen table, but Mother Pratt intercepted them, saying, "Right you two, go and wash your hands."

"My hands are clean," came a moan from Dennis.

"I don't think so!" Vicky said to Dennis on Mother's behalf. "You've picked up dirt in the garden that can't be seen."

"You mean bacteria," Dennis answered back. "Is that what dirt is that can't be seen?" he asked his mother. "Is that what Vicky means?"

Dennis waited for an answer but none came, as Mother Pratt was busy buttering the toast and her mind sort of heard the question and sort of did not. Mother Pratt then repeated her orders, as mothers so often do.

"Go upstairs and wash, please! And tell your father his cup of tea is brewing."

Maisy, Daisy and Duncan were left to roam the garden with Bounder, who had only nibbled at his food (as cats often do!) wanting to keep a cat's eye on them, but he planned to pop back into the kitchen when Vicky and Dennis came back down. Unfortunately, the Pratt family didn't get to see the dragonflies who were Faeries sitting upon the rabbits' heads. If only they'd looked out the window!

The flapping wings of the dragonflies made music that only the rabbits could hear. The frogs began croaking and the finches began singing along with the sparrows, and the sweet cooing of doves and pigeons was also heard. Even the crows joined in with their cawing, but not their usual shrieking caws; their call was soft and gentle, sounding like a drumbeat in the background.

The back garden became full of bright light again much like someone turning on a switch. The dragonfly Faeries were speaking to Duncan who relayed the information to the Angels, because in the daytime it wasn't as easy for the Faeries and Angels to speak to each other. This was because of the busy activity in the world which blocked out their ability to fully communicate, but the Angels knew that Duncan was still able to speak with both them and the Faeries. He was a go-between for the Angels and the Faeries, kind of like a transmitter. Duncan was like a telephone in the Faerie world!

Inside the Pratt house, Vicky and Dennis, having a big appetite after playing outside, gobbled the hot brown toast that was spread with their mother's homemade jam and marmalade. Father Jim sipped his tea and glanced through the newspaper after greeting Vicky and Dennis with a very happy and loud, "Good morning children!"

Mother Pratt was by the stove preparing scrambled eggs for everyone, as Molly sat on the floor next to Vicky's chair, washing her face with her paws, carefully cleaning the dust away from her fur. Mother Pratt said to Vicky and Dennis,

"After breakfast your father is going to drive us to town and we are going to buy you each a new pair of summer shoes."

"Ahh!" Vicky and Dennis groaned together.

Dennis said, "We want to stay in the garden today to play with the rabbits and the cats!"

Vicky stroked Molly's head as she was now very comfortably curled up on Vicky's lap looking up at her friend. "Molly has already told me that she wants me to stay!"

"I thought you would enjoy shopping for shoes," said Mother Pratt. "And please, Vicky, stop saying that Molly is speaking to you! You are getting too old to be saying things like that now. And get Molly off your knee while you are eating, please."

Dennis, busy licking the remains of the very tasty jam off his fingers said, "They want some food too Mom! Look at Bounder, he's staring at me waiting for a treat!"

Bounder had again returned from doing his guard duty in the garden, hoping to get a little more food.

"I have fed the cats already, Dennis," Mother Pratt said. "So don't go feeding Bounder anything from the table."

But Vicky had already jumped up to get the cats their special treats from the box in the cupboard and Mother Pratt didn't say a word. She really loved Bounder and Molly and her own mothering instinct wanted to spoil them as well.

"I have fed the cats already, Dennis," Mother Pratt said. "So don't go feeding Bounder anything from the table."

Father Jim had been the only quiet one at the breakfast table. He didn't usually interfere with Mother Pratt's rules and so let her make the plans for the day. He got up to fill his mug with more tea and while doing so, he leaned over and kissed Dennis on the head while kissing Vicky on her cheek.

"We won't be long shopping," he said, folding the corner of the newspaper and placing it on the table. "We will be back in a few hours at most. I need the car this week for work so it has to be today. It's a bank holiday today and all the shops are open." He waited for any signs of protest from the kids. When none came he said, satisfied, "Good! Now let's all go out and enjoy ourselves and have some fun. At lunchtime we will go to the fish and chip shop." That suited Dennis just fine.

"Jim," Mother Pratt said as she wiped her hands dry after washing the last breakfast dish. "Have you by any chance seen my red shoe? I found one on the bedroom floor but the other has gone completely missing. I just don't know where it could be, I've looked all over."

"Sorry love," Father Jim replied. "I haven't come across the likes of a missing red shoe." He held his head, as if he was thinking about something important, then said with excitement in his voice,

"Wait a moment! Isn't that out of a storybook? Didn't someone else lose a red shoe?" Father Jim continued, as he loved more than anything to make jokes, even if they were corny, as they so often were. "Perhaps my dear, you will soon be going to a ball of some sort."

Jim began laughing, although Mother Pratt wasn't overly amused. However, Father Jim continued with his story.

"But the question is Sue, will you be taking me? Because as I remember how the story went, Cinderella was looking for a date, or something like that!"

"Oh, James, don't be so silly!" Mother Sue flicked her tea towel at him.

Father Jim liked being silly. He enjoyed behaving like a child at times, for it made him feel happy and carefree, reminding him of how he used to be when he was young. Although Father Jim looked serious at times, inside, he wasn't serious at all. He was a great thinker (like Duncan the rabbit), and had deep conversations with himself about his plans but he was always able to laugh at himself.

"Dad!" Vicky said. "Cinderella wasn't looking for a date. She was looking to meet her prince at the ball and her wicked stepsisters were trying to keep her away. They treated her very badly and with so much hate! Mom isn't like that."

"You never know, love," Father Jim said, winking at Vicky. "There's a lot you don't know about your mother. She's a dark horse, she is. Didn't she tell you how it was growing up with her sisters?"

"What do you mean?" Vicky asked, surprised by what her father said. "Are you saying that Aunt Emma and Aunt Angie were nasty to Mummy?"

"Oh Jim," Mother Pratt said. "Don't be making up stories for Vicky and Dennis to repeat. You don't want Vicky having bad thoughts about Emma and Angie." Mother Sue gently brushed a strand of loose hair away from Vicky's eyes. "Of course, you know that's not true, Vicky."

Father Jim went off to the living room, smiling and tucking the newspaper under one arm while holding his cup of tea in his other hand. He was going to check in on their budgie, Pretty Boy, who was patiently waiting to be fed and let out of his cage. Pretty Boy enjoyed flying around the house, chirping happily, and loved to dart around Bounder and Molly who never tried to attack him as they like Pretty Boy.

Mother Sue had taught Pretty Boy to speak, and when she sat in the living room, he would talk away in his shrill voice as sat perched on her head. This was quite funny to watch Mother Pratt reading the newspaper, eyeglasses resting on the bridge of her nose, and Pretty Boy leaning down towards the paper as though he was reading it along with her!

28

When the television was on, Pretty Boy would flutter about in front of the picture tube, having his own conversation with the voices on the telly. At other times when he was sitting on the ledge of the windowsill looking out the window, and saw a bird or dog passing by, he would suddenly shout,

"Look at the birdies! Look at the doggies!"

Pretty Boy had light blue and dark green feathers with a white patch under his chin. He was only two years-old, and was very much a part of the family, especially during the evening time when they sat together watching television. On warm sunny days, Mother Sue would take Pretty Boy outside in the back garden in his cage, but it was far too dangerous for him to be let out. Pretty Boy had keen eyes. He could see the Angels and the Faeries darting to and fro, as the Faeries flickered their Faerie dust on Maisy, Daisy and Duncan. He would scream out in his budgie voice, repeating over and over again, "Look at the Angels! Look at the Faeries!"

Nobody in the Pratt household thought this was an odd thing for him to be saying.

CHAPTER THREE

Off to the shops

After breakfast, Vicky and Dennis had their showers and brushed their teeth, and after much ado the family was ready to go shopping. The rabbits were put back in their hutches and the cats were free to roam in and out of the house. They were able to use the cat flap on the back of the kitchen door, which Father Jim had put in, when he had a day of remembering work projects.

Mother Pratt, neatly dressed in her dark green slacks and white cotton blouse, was struggling to open the passenger door of the car. The busy street outside was filled with whooshing sounds of passing traffic. After many tries without succeeding, Mother Pratt began to lose her patience. The car was getting old and had a few dents on the passenger door, making it difficult at times to open or shut easily. She gave one final pull with all her strength and finally the door opened with a loud creak.

"Thank Goodness!" she said as she straightened her blouse, making a mental note of another job James definitely needed to do.

Although the day had started out bright and warm with only a slight breeze, the wind had now picked up, whipping pieces of paper and debris all over the street. The weather was quickly changing.

When everyone finally got into the car, Dennis said from the backseat. "I need to go the toilet."

"Oh Dennis. Why didn't you go before?" Mother Pratt said with a bit of irritation in her voice.

"I did Mummy! I did go before. But now I need to go some more."

Mother Pratt once again jiggled with the door handle but Vicky held out her hand towards her mother, saying in her best adult voice, "Give me the key, Mother. I'll let Dennis in the front door, as I want to get a sweater that's in my drawer."

Mother Pratt said, "Very well, Vicky. Here's the key, but make sure you slam the door hard so it will lock. You know how it sticks and doesn't always shut tight."

Father Jim sat in the driver's seat absentmindedly fiddling with his mobile phone, going through his address book for one reason or another, and said, "Get going now, Dennis. I'll start the car and wait for you."

But Vicky and Dennis had already left the car when he spoke and didn't hear what their father said. Father Jim probably wouldn't have heard their answer anyway as he was back to fiddling with his mobile phone.

Vicky grabbed her brother by the hand, acting like a mother, pulling him towards the front door. For a change, Dennis didn't resist. As they ran towards the door dark clouds were blowing in and the air was suddenly getting cooler.

Totally wrapped up in his mobile phone, Father Jim forgot to start the car. He was in the process of sending a text message to his friend about the Alsatian dog he had rescued from a nearby neighbour. This dog had the saddest look that Jim had ever seen. There didn't seem to be any light in his eyes and he was as lonely as anyone could be.

The dog was chained day and night to the gate of the neighbour's fence to keep out trespassers, so this "poor dog" (Mother Sue's expression) was without any company. The owners didn't care much for the dog at all. They gave him food and water but left him outside to be on his own. They only wanted him to protect their valuable antique furniture, locked in their old garage.

This being their money-making business, it was important that no thieves would think to break in when they saw a Beware of Dog sign on the fence and then the dog.

After many weeks of passing by the house, Father Jim could no longer bear seeing the dog looking so sad and lonely. It bothered him so much that he found it difficult to concentrate on his work.

He decided to go to the animal shelter and explain the circumstances to the RSPCA, hoping they would investigate, which they did. What they discovered was that the neighbours had made a habit of keeping other dogs chained up and alone when they lived elsewhere. This was not acceptable to Jim and he asked the inspectors,

"Why have a guard dog only and not a dog who would be first your friend?"

The dog was only three or four years old, but he looked well over ten, having spent all those years living by himself with no one to pet him, say kind words to him, or even take him for a walk. The inspectors, not liking what they saw in the neighbours' backyard, released the dog from its chained post and took him away to the shelter. He even licked them when they approached him to cut the chain. He wasn't mean at all!

That same day, Jim called his friend, Charlie, to tell him about "the poor dog" (Mother Sue's words), and Charlie drove straight to the RSPCA shelter that evening and paid the fees. He took the dog home to begin a new life in the country where he and his family live. The family called him Benjy and he now runs and plays with the horses and other animals on Charlie's small farm. Benjy changed back to the young dog that he was, proving again that the energy of love surely does work!

"Father Jim," Vicky would proudly say when retelling this story to Dennis in front of their animal friends, "Is a kind and loving man."

And the three rabbits, Molly and Bounder, the Faeries and the Angels as well, applauded in silent agreement for a job well done.

****

Some hours had passed by as the Pratt family walked up and down the shopping centre, buying what was needed and some things that weren't, one thing leading to another.

Vicky and Dennis had forgotten, for a few minutes at least, their wonderful garden and their beloved pets, as they were having fun. Dennis was discovering new toys to play with, feasting his eyes on a model airplane. He loved watching the planes circling the sky around his home, wishing he could be up there looking down on the world. That would be even more of an adventure than climbing to the top of the beech tree, and much more exciting too! Dennis dreamed of being a pilot one day.

Vicky and her mother had spent some time in a crystal bead shop that had hundreds of coloured glass beads, as well as real gemstones. Some sparkled, some glittered, some were so tiny that they were barely big enough to thread and others were large enough to be worn around the neck as a beautiful pendant.

"Oh! How I would love to make a necklace for mummy!" Vicky said to herself out loud, as she looked through the tray on top of the glass counter. "With that bead and that beautiful one too."

The saleswoman smiled at Vicky, and gave her five yellow amber beads to take home. She said it was a stone that brought good fortune and should be worn on a string around the neck. Vicky's eyes lit up, and she thanked the lady. Mother Pratt also thanked her, and then bought some leather cord for the beads and two pendants that had sun signs for Vicky and Dennis.

Vicky was a Virgo and Dennis a Gemini. Mother Pratt had decided to spend a little more money today than was originally planned, so shopping for shoes became a bigger event that everyone enjoyed.

Father Jim spent most of his time in the electronics shop looking over all the new gadgets. He was reading information about the different televisions and new types of mobile phones, as well as giving the new computers a long look-over. This was his kind of place!

After the shopping was over, the family stopped at the fish and chip shop before returning home. Vicky and Dennis couldn't believe that Father Jim and Mother Sue ordered a curry sauce to pour over their chips. "Ugh!" Dennis blurted out, as he put vinegar and ketchup on his. "This is what normal people put on their chips." He said, teasing his parents.

Don't you know by now, Dennis, that Mom and Dad aren't normal, especially Dad!" The Pratt family all laughed

Everyone was tired yet quite happy and content when they drove up to a parking spot just in front of their front door. That is, until they discovered the front door was wide open and clanging back and forth due to the gusting wind that was blowing. Dark clouds had now covered the sun, and the air had a chill that said rain was on its way.

"Vicky!" Mother Pratt said with concerned alarm in her voice. "You didn't shut the door properly."

"I thought I closed it tight. I thought I'd shut the door with all my might." Vicky said with a sinking feeling in her stomach, hoping that Bounder and Molly didn't go out. The front area was off limits for them.

"Oh dear," Father Jim could only say.

CHAPTER FOUR

Molly's missing

A feeling of fear surrounded the Pratt family at that moment, making Mother Pratt scold her daughter. It was the energy of fear, fear of the unknown, fear of what the open door could mean. What they were all thinking but not saying was, "Did the cats venture out the open front door?" Vicky ran into the house to search for them, with Dennis and their mother following right behind.

Father Jim was trying to distract his mind from the wave of fearful energy that made him feel worried, so he looked up and studied the sky, wondering if the dark clouds would bring much rain or whether the gusting wind might blow them right by. The continuous banging of the front door brought Jim back from any further daydreaming, and he walked slowly up the steps leading to the house expecting trouble. This was not only Jim's worried mind, but was also his intuition. It is what he felt inside his tummy even though his mind tried to wish it away.

"Molly! Molly! Molly!" Vicky yelled with panic in her voice. When she entered the house, she'd immediately seen Bounder sitting by the windowsill, quiet and staring outside. Molly was not with him like she usually was. Vicky went off to the other rooms shouting Molly's name over and over again, but there was no sign of her, not even a meow.

Dennis was greatly relieved when he saw Bounder, but

35

remained worried when not seeing Molly. A stabbing fear touched his heart.

Vicky ran down the stairs after looking in all the bedrooms, tears beginning to stream down her face. "Molly's not in the house," she said to Mother Pratt and Dennis.

Mother Pratt tried to remain calm with Vicky as Father Jim slowly walked into the house. Mother Pratt glanced at him with nervous eyes, then turned to Vicky and said, "Let's look in the back garden, love. Molly is most probably there on top of the rabbit hutch."

But Molly wasn't there. She was missing.

The rabbits knew Molly was missing as they lay still in their hutches buried in the straw. They felt the missing energy and felt Molly's fear as well. Bounder knew quite well what was up. It was why he was sitting so still by the window. Energy, as Duncan would say, travels very far. Bounder had seen Molly creep through the open front door and had watched her crawl ever so slowly into the tiny front garden. Bounder watched how Molly did indeed get into trouble.

When Molly was in the front garden she began at first to sniff at the beautiful roses and yellow dandelions. Bounder heard her say, "I'll just smell these pretty flowers for a bit."

But curiosity took over, as Molly then peeked her head through one of the open spaces of the wooden picket fence, and then seeing directly in front of her an old blue van with the back door wide open. At that moment Bounder had hissed loudly through the window to warn her not to go there. But Molly didn't heed him and Bounder heard her say,

"I wonder what's inside? I think I shall just take a little look."

Molly jumped first onto the bumper of the van and then ever so slowly crept into the van, without any thought of danger. Once inside, curiosity again took hold of her, as she began to investigate, walking around the boxes and different types of steel objects which she didn't know were tools. From the window, Bounder saw Molly disappear from sight and he cried out with a loud, "Meow!" so Molly could hear him, but when curiosity took over Molly, it usually blocked out everything else.

The van belonged to a man who repaired faulty electrics in houses. Molly's curiosity and great interest in all the boxes and little hiding spots came to a halt when she finally heard Bounder's warning, which sent shivers up and down her spine. Molly immediately began to crawl her way back around the boxes, but just as she was ready to jump out, she heard the rusty squeak of the van's back doors and they slammed shut, trapping Molly inside. The electrical man had finished his job!

A wave of panic overtook Molly and she backed away from the back doors and scrambled behind the boxes near the driver's seat. Had she only cried out, the electrical man would have set her free, but all Molly could do was cower in fear. It was this fearful energy that prevented her from being released.

Molly wished she had listened to Bounder and then she thought about Vicky and how alone she was without her best friend nearby to save her. Molly could feel thoughts coming from Maisy, Daisy and Duncan as well, who knew at that moment Molly was in danger. How? They just knew, especially Duncan. Molly realized how silly she was to have jumped into the van, and if she had been less curious she would still be at home, safe in the back garden.

The van drove away into a busier part of town. The electrician hummed away to a song on the radio as he drove and then began to slow down to park by the next house he was going to work at. There was a moment of silence when he turned the engine off, which helped Molly to calm down and gather her thoughts. She wisely crept towards the back doors, planning to jump out when the electrician opened them.

Her intuition was spot on, as the electrical man opened the van's back doors just as quickly as he had closed them before. Molly saw the light of day when the electrician reached for his toolbox, she leapt from the van onto the paved road. She jumped as fast as a blink of the eye. The electrical man didn't notice a thing as he closed the doors with a rickety squeak and a loud thump. Molly heard the whooshing sound of cars passing by and felt a swirling wind ruffle against her fur.

Molly escapes from Rob's electrical van

"Where am I?" she wondered, looking every which way, searching for cover from the buzzing traffic and finding none. "Where am I?" she asked again, this time letting out a loud cry which sounded like a shriek.

The loud noises of the traffic hurt her ears, frightening her as panic crept in. She ran across the street, barely missing the tire of a passing car. Two other cars braked just in time to avoid hitting her, the screeching noise of tires almost making Molly freeze on the spot - in the middle of the busy two-way road! Luckily she was not squashed by a car, for Molly had the Angels watching over her. They pushed her with a surge of energy, like a puff of wind, to make her legs run faster to get all the way across the busy street.

A red bus came within inches of hitting her furry body, in

fact the tip of her tail brushed against the tires as it whizzed by, but Molly kept on running. That she made the crossing was a miracle.

Someone had to be watching over her and they were, the Angels and the Faeries were with her. Duncan in his hutch was biting frantically at the tiny wires of his cage. He knew of the dangers Molly had just faced

"Go this way my darling!" the Angels whispered in her ear. "Run to this side and then down that narrow path, quickly now! Quickly!"

A giant pit bull leaped out at Molly, barking fiercely, but the chain he was attached to tugged at his neck and he couldn't go any further. Molly didn't have time to be relieved or thankful that the dog was chained up. She was too busy turning this way, that way and every which way, as the Angels kept guiding her until at long last she found her frightened and tired body facing the entrance of a large park full of trees and bushes. Without hesitation, Molly squeezed her panting body under the hedges.

"I am so afraid!" she said to herself, shaking so much that sweat soaked her fur. "What am I to do?"

Molly was in shock and remained motionless. All her thoughts were on getting back to Vicky. But which way was home? Molly heard the voices of children shouting as they played in the open field of the park, and saw human adults out walking their dogs, thankfully not too close by. Molly sat hidden in the bushes, trembling with fear, wishing she had not been so foolish and wishing that she was back at home.

****

Meanwhile, back at the Pratt house, hours had passed by with Vicky and her family searching everywhere for Molly, with no success. They had looked up and down the street countless times, through lane-ways and into the back gardens of other people's homes. They called and called her name, but there was no answer from Molly.

Vicky now lay in her bed crying quietly, the salty tears stinging her eyes with Bounder curled beside her. Bounder knew his presence would comfort Vicky a little, and Dennis lay on his bed beside Vicky's in silence, staring out the window watching stormy clouds blow in, much as his father had.

Mother Pratt and Father Jim knew there was a good chance that Molly might have been run down by a car if she had dared to cross their busy street. They were getting more concerned as the hours passed by without any sign of Molly. They were thinking, without saying a word, that it was quite possible that Molly was not alive. Worry and sadness filled their hearts.

But Molly's three rabbit friends, Maisy, Daisy and especially Duncan, along with Bounder, knew different. They knew Molly was alive. They sensed these things much more than humans. Duncan knew Molly was in the park hiding in the bushes, frightened but safe for the time being. Maisy and Daisy huddled close to each other listening to Duncan in the hutch above them speak his thoughts to the Angels.

"You must go to Molly and comfort her," he said. "Tell her that she must remain hidden where she is. She is safe there."

The Angels told Duncan that there was so much commotion going on in the human world that it interfered with communication between them and the Faeries. They told Duncan that he must give the Faeries a message, which was, 'When evening comes, Molly must leave the hedges where she is hiding.'

Duncan's large ears twitched a mile a minute, as he received messages from the Angels, sending them to the Faerie world.

The Angels continued to speak to Duncan, saying, "Molly must climb up the oak tree that is right near her and she must do this very soon, so she can hide overnight in the branches amongst the leaves." Duncan thumped his foot in approval.

"Trees are good and safe," he replied. "Good and safe."

"We will help Vicky and Dennis in their dreams tonight to let them know where Molly is. The Faeries will be with us as well. We will tell Vicky and Dennis that Molly is alive. They will know where she is and they will believe!"

The Angels flickered over Duncan's head, one landing on his back, feeling like a feather tickling him.

"Father and Mother Pratt do not hear us very well," the Angels all spoke in one voice. "Their doubts block out hope and without hope there is nothing to believe. Father Pratt is a little more open, but not enough yet to believe in our messages. Vicky and Dennis will listen. Duncan," the Angels said to him in singsong voices.

"Tell the Faeries to go to Molly now and give her hope, and this will remove her fear. The Faeries can do this."

So Duncan relayed the message from the Angels to the Faeries, twitching his nose excitedly as he communicated each detail. When he finished, the Faeries, who at that moment had been butterflies flicked their wings together and immediately changed into dragonflies. They then flew high into the sky and from a distance they looked like a hoard of bees headed for their hive.

Dennis had been looking out the window at that moment and was amazed, for he had never seen so many dragonflies in his life, all flying together. He wondered what was going on outside by the rabbit hutch. His intuition told him that perhaps something good was about to happen!

So Duncan relayed the message from the Angels to the Faeries, twitching his nose excitedly as he communicated each detail.

CHAPTER FIVE

A simple plan

That night, the Angels and Faeries had a plan. They were going to talk with Vicky and Dennis in their dreams. Vicky and Dennis were in for a special treat.

The dragonfly Faeries, who had been lovely butterflies, were moving fast and furious after flying over the Pratt house. Zooming around the busy street, they passed over the heads of many people who as usual were rushing about, as humans always do when outside their homes. The human adults just had too many things going on in their life to notice that the dragonfly Faeries hovered above them, although a number children and babies in their strollers did see them.

Adults walking in the path of the dragonflies only heard a loud buzzing noise that tingled in their ears, which they impatiently tried to rub away with their hands. Others swatted at their hair as the dragonflies swooshed by, not knowing that it wasn't just the wind blowing. It was a shame that the adults couldn't speak to each other the way Duncan and his friends could, because if they did, they would have been able to share their thoughts about having the same buzzing noise experience. They would have found out there was a lot more going on than they thought. The sad thing is that humans have always been able to speak to each other with their thoughts, but have forgotten how. They could still be able to if only they believed.

The Grumps (grown-ups) have stopped believing and they expect their children to do the same, which is very sad indeed.

The Faeries told Duncan that the elves were really another part of the Faerie world, helping with all things. The Sidhe (pronounced Shee) look after the plant world and the Faeries work with them as well. The Sidhe are twelve feet tall but now have to hide from humans, for people would be afraid of their size and try to harm them, thinking them bad or mean. The human adults are so wrong. The Sidhe are actually very understanding and the kindest of beings. So the Sidhe decided to become invisible and live underground, putting all their concern and attention towards the plants and trees. They, of course still work with the Angels and Faeries when called upon.

The Angels and Faeries have much work to do with the human adults, knowing that everyone is born with hope and belief in their hearts. Belief is what love is, for when you love someone, you actually believe in them as much as you believe in yourself. Hope and belief bring happiness to everyone and this was what the Angels and the Faeries were going to bring to the Pratt house during the night. But first, the dragonfly Faeries were going to bring hope to Molly.

Everyone in the Pratt house was feeling sad about Molly's disappearance, but it was still mixed with hope and a belief that she would be found. A glimmer of hope is about the same size as the tiny specks of light that the Angels brought to the back garden which can get bigger and brighter. Sadness and sorrow are like specks of dark cloud which can become larger than the specks of light if you allow it to, much like dark clouds blocking the sunlight.

Vicky and Dennis had more hope about Molly returning home than their parents did. Since Mother Sue and Father Jim were older, they had of course experienced more disappointment in their lives. As more time went by without Molly showing up, they were beginning to expect the worst, even though they kept their voices silent and their thoughts to themselves. They continued speaking to Vicky with hopeful words rather than creating more worry.

"Don't fret, Vicky darling," Mother Sue said to her. "Molly might still turn up at the door." She hugged her daughter, brushing her tears away. "Or she might be in some person's house at this very moment. You never know dear."

Vicky didn't believe Molly would be in another person's house. That wasn't her way.

"We shall see what tomorrow brings. Won't we, love?" said Father Jim.

Vicky, with a heavy heart, walked quietly upstairs to her bedroom and lay on her bed, looking out her window and saying out loud, "Oh where could Molly be?"

****

Dennis went into the back garden to sit with the rabbits. The wind had stopped blowing and once again the birds began to chirp their happy songs. "Perhaps the storm was passing over," thought Dennis, which would be safer for Molly, wherever she was. He kept eyeing the sky, not looking at the clouds this time but searching for dragonflies, and in doing so missed the tiny bright lights from the Angels floating about the rabbit hutches.

It was at that exact time that the bright green dragonflies entered the park. They had breezed by the lane where the chained-up pit bull was, and zoomed into the bushes beside the oak tree where Molly was hiding. She had not moved an inch.

Molly was relieved to see the dragonfly Faeries, knowing right away who they were. She immediately felt hope inside, washing away her fear and loneliness, and with that change of energy, Molly became lighthearted. The dragonflies had indeed brought light and hope.

The Faeries spoke to Molly, through the energy of their thoughts, telling her that the hedges would not be safe for her later. They told Molly to climb the oak tree beside the hedges and find a strong branch with many leaves for cover, and to wait for Vicky to come to her, for she would. The Faeries told Molly she would be home by tomorrow night.

Molly began to purr hearing the message the Faeries had given her. She began to think that she might make it home after all, and this gave to her a great feeling inside, that feeling of hope. The thought of returning home to Vicky, Dennis and Bounder and of course the rabbits, made her feel extremely happy. Home was where her heart was.

The dragonflies swirled around the hedges, staying near Molly and protecting the area until evening began to creep in. Then it was time to climb the tree.

Molly scrambled up the oak tree with her sharp claws, something she was quite good at doing, and found a branch that was sturdy and safe. The dragonflies swarmed around, dusting her coat with Faerie dust to protect her. Molly sat like a bird on a branch hidden and content.

Molly sat like a bird on a branch hidden and content.

She was no longer afraid. The dark clouds threatening to bring rain all afternoon had been pushed completely away by the wind, and the sky that was covered in darkness was now clear. To Molly, the morning in the garden with Vicky and Dennis and all of her friends seemed like such a long, long time ago.

Bounder lay with Vicky on her bed when he suddenly felt the energy change and he knew, without knowing how, that Molly was safe and he knew, again without knowing how, that she would be back. Bounder, as most cats can, directed this good feeling towards Vicky and she began to feel lighter and more at peace, although she didn't understand why.

Maisy and Daisy and Duncan felt the energy change as well, and like Bounder did with Vicky, they sent their good feelings towards Dennis, who was lying on the grass staring up at the clearing sky, watching the clouds move further and further away. He thought it was like a miracle, because usually when such storm clouds as these rolled in from the coast, they brought rain.

Pretty Boy was flitting about the living room of the Pratt house and he felt this change of energy as well. The feelings of hope and light came to him from Bounder and the rabbits. He began to chirp and whistle, which helped soothe Father Jim and Mother Sue's nerves while they sat on the couch watching the telly. They weren't really watching the telly though, as they were caught in their thoughts, waiting and hoping for somebody to phone, after letting many of their neighbours know about Molly's disappearance.

For Pretty Boy to be excited and happy at this particular time was a sign, a good one, so thought Father Jim, although he couldn't figure out the reason why.

****

With life down on Earth, the Angels and Faeries are not allowed to change the course of events for humans, but they can still offer help, especially when they are asked. It's the same for animals, fish, birds or even snakes - for all living creatures.

The rivers, lakes, plants, trees and even rocks have life energy.

Changing someone's direction or choosing a different, or better way for someone without them knowing or asking, would be to interfere with the plan of the universe because at certain times, everyone has to learn to make their own decisions.

The Angels are allowed to help in other ways, by sending messages through dreams, or sometimes through thoughts that seem to appear in our heads out of nowhere. All we need to do is remain open.

This is why the Angels couldn't pick Molly up from the oak tree and bring her home, which would seem to be the fastest and easiest way. They are capable of doing this, but are not allowed to do so. Down here on Earth, everybody has to learn certain things for themselves.

The Angels were going to speak to Dennis and Vicky through their dreams that night and tell them where Molly was. They were still open enough to believe, and because of that, they would be able to understand how energy really worked.

Vicky and Dennis only needed to know that Molly was alive and safe in the oak tree in the park, and where the park was. The rest they would have to figure out; how to get to Molly and rescue her. The Angels knew exactly what they were going to do as soon as nighttime arrived.

After Dennis had finished feeding the rabbits fresh lettuce, carrots and some tiny grain pellets, and locked them safely in their hutches, he went up to bed after saying goodnight to

Mother Sue and Father Jim, who were still watching the telly with Pretty Boy.

Vicky was almost asleep when Dennis came into their room. She was curled up under her favourite pink cotton blanket and murmured goodnight to Dennis, adding,

"Goodnight Molly, wherever you are." Burying her head into her feather pillow she closed her tired, tear-stained eyes and fell into a deep sleep.

It didn't take long for Dennis to also drift off to sleep for when Mother Sue came up to tuck them in shortly after, they were both sound asleep. She kissed them goodnight and gently closed the door, going back downstairs to sit with Father Jim who was snoring on the couch with Pretty Boy sitting on his head. Mother Sue had to chuckle at that. She decided it was best that she and Jim go to bed early and so she clicked off the television and brought Pretty Boy back to his cage.

Father Jim was snoring on the couch with Pretty Boy sitting on his head

It was time for the Angels to work their magic.

When Mother Sue closed Vicky and Dennis's bedroom door, the Angels immediately arrived and sprinkled specks of dust around the room. This is what we all wake up to in the morning, when we have the corners of our eyes filled with what seems to be sand. When Dennis had said upon waking that morning, "The sandman came during the night," he was close to the truth, although it was only a half-truth, for it was really the Angels who had come and dusted their room.

49

The Faeries were also with the Angels in their bedroom singing in very low, humming voices, so low that even if you were sitting in a chair wide awake in their bedroom, you wouldn't have heard them.

The Faeries in Dennis and Vicky's room had a very different look than the dragonfly Faeries who were with Molly in the oak tree. These Faeries were much smaller and lit up every few seconds just like fireflies. In fact, they were fireflies and they filled the room with their bright flashes. Dark blues, bright pinks and deep green sparks of light made Vicky and Dennis's dark room glow like a rainbow.

Bounder stared at the flickering lights without moving a muscle, his orange front paws tucked securely against his chest. His tail would occasionally flip one way to the other as Faerie dust fell upon his fur. The dusting in Vicky and Dennis's room was a way to sooth them while they slept. It was protection from bad dreams, which is why Dreamcatchers are helpful. Vicky had a dreamcatcher perfectly placed on the wall above her and Dennis's bed.

The sweet lullaby music coming from the Angels brought smiles to the sleeping faces of Vicky and Dennis. Bounder lay on Dennis's bed and felt so good with the energy coming from the Angels and Faeries that he began to purr quite contently.

Vicky had already begun her dream, and in it she was seeing her grandmother who had passed away two years ago. Mother Pratt was still sad about this. Grandma was now telling Vicky in her dream how truly happy she was, being back in the spirit world with Grandpa and all her friends. This is what we call heaven.

Grandma told Vicky that she often came to visit them in their house and spoke to them at times, although they couldn't hear her. Grandma said she kept careful watch over Vicky and her family.

"There are so many interesting things about my new life with the Angels," Grandma was saying.

"Vicky darling," she continued. "When we get older, we stop believing in the true miracles of life. I have come to see that this is so wrong and quite sad. You see dear, your mother is sad about my leaving your world. She is so busy with you and Dennis and your Daddy, she forgets to see or feel that I am still with her. She has forgotten to believe." Grandma carried on speaking to Vicky in a soft, soothing voice.

"You can show her how to believe, my dear. This I will tell you later, but first I want to give you news of your precious Molly. I want you to know..." Grandma leaned closer to Vicky's ear, whispering to her... "I want you to know that Molly is alive and waiting for you to come to her. I will show you where she is in your dreams and you will see her for yourself and believe. So no need for any more tears, my sweet, Vicky. You will be with your Molly tomorrow."

She kissed her granddaughter's forehead, which felt to Vicky like a warm gentle breeze touching her face, as a new dream entered her mind. In it, Vicky saw Molly sleeping on a branch with the dragonfly Faeries resting beside her. It was night, but Vicky could see so clearly it seemed like daytime. That's how dreams are sometimes.

"Molly is in the park, Vicky," her grandma gently said. She stroked Vicky's head as she faded in and out of Vicky's dream. "I must go now, my love," Grandma said. "And visit with your brother, Dennis. When you awake tomorrow, you must ask the electrician, who will be working next door, where he drove to after his job here. His name is Rob. He will direct you to Molly because there is a park near the house that he drove to for his other job. He will tell you." Grandma's voice was fading.

"Molly is in the big oak tree in the park," she repeated. "The big oak tree in the park.

****

Grandma left Vicky's dream, as the Angels now sent her to

visit Dennis, who was already in his dream world and talking to Duncan with Maisy and Daisy nearby. Duncan's nose was twitching rather quickly and his back paw thumped with each word he said, as he was telling Dennis that Molly was waiting for Vicky to come and fetch her in the park.

"Vicky knows which park," said Duncan as Maisy and Daisy snuggled up around Dennis's neck and ear, tickling him, making him laugh.

"You are a good boy, Dennis. Maisy and Daisy and I love you very much. You are young, but are learning so much about life because you are beginning to know that everything has feelings and feelings are really energy. Remember that you can talk to the flowers in your garden and they will be able to hear you and that is why they blossom more than other flowers because they are happier when you send them good thoughts. The frogs in your pond feel the same way, as all living things do. Everything in this world has life.

"The rocks have energy as well, Dennis, and that is why Maisy, Daisy and I thumped our back legs when you threw the rock into the water-pond. The rock didn't want to be disturbed from its old home and thrown into the water which scared the frogs. So, tomorrow if you want, you can go back to the pond and return the rock to its home. It will be very happy to once again sit in the sun where it has purpose. That rock is very old, and protects the garden with its ancient memory. Rocks can do that.

"Trees," Duncan continued in Dennis's dream, "have the energy of life in their roots and through that energy, their branches can speak to each other. Leaves that fall from the branches die, but in spring the buds begin to blossom and new leaves form once again in the same places where the old leaves lived. It is the same with your grandmother, Dennis. Grandma has only moved to another place on her journey, as her soul is like the bud on the tree."

Duncan's voice became silent in Dennis's dream as he,

Maisy and Daisy began to fade away. In their hutches, Maisy and Daisy were in a deep sleep, snug as bugs, cuddled together and Duncan was sound asleep in his hutch above them.

Grandma now appeared in Dennis' dream. Dennis was at her house, drinking a glass of cold milk and eating a piece of her homemade chocolate cake, and did it ever taste good! He was really happy to be with his Grandma, as he watched her baking his favourite, oatmeal raisin biscuits.

Grandma told Dennis, "Your mother's red shoe is underneath her bureau. Tell her, Dennis love, that I told you this in a dream. Your mother needs to believe again, dear, but she will want to have proof to make her believe. Adults always need proof for one reason or another." Dennis took another bite of the delicious cake and kept listening.

"Remind her also, Dennis, that when she was your age she found an old teddy bear sitting in a rubbish bin and she took the teddy home, washed it and mended its wounds and slept with him every night for years. She would whisper and share all her secrets with Teddy, secrets she never told anyone, nor did she think anyone knew what she shared with him. But I know now, Dennis. I know now.

"You see sweetheart, by telling you what I know, this will be her proof." Grandma took the tray of biscuits from the oven and they smelled delicious as she put them in front of Dennis. She continued, "Tell your mother that her favourite watch, the one your father gave her at Christmas, the one that stopped working five years ago and couldn't bear to throw away, is now working. You tell her you know it is in her second bureau drawer beside her red sweater. Her favourite watch is now working, Dennis, love. You can tell your mother all these things tomorrow.

"It will take her some time to believe Vicky's story, when she says she knows where Molly is as she will want to have her proof. You can then tell her what I said to you in your dreams. Tomorrow, your mother will start believing again but it will take a bit of time" Smiling at Dennis, who had his face covered with chocolate, Grandma finished by saying,

"I am so glad you enjoyed your cake and biscuits, sweetheart, but now you must go back to sleep and I will come visit you again, soon. Sleep well, my dear child, sleep well." Blowing a kiss to Dennis, Grandma disappeared from his dream.

****

The Faeries sang their beautiful songs well into the night and the Angels shone rays of blue light across the faces of Vicky and Dennis.

Everyone in the house, including Pretty Boy, slept extremely well that night. The Angels, along with Grandma, came into Father Jim and Mother Sue's dreams as well, sprinkling dust on their bed and upon their faces, leaving them peacefully smiling in their sleep.

What Grandma told her daughter were private matters, to help mend her heart. She told Mother Sue that she must start believing again as this was really why she was feeling sad. Grandma spoke about the energy of moths and that finding moths in the house was very lucky indeed, because they were symbols of money, and that it was good that the children saved the moths from her broom.

"Wait and see, love," she patted Sue's head. "You will come to know that I am right about this and about many other things."

Jim had been flying in his dreams when Grandma appeared to him. She took him by the hand and guided him around to his old neighbourhood, the one he grew up in. He was pleased to see Grandma and hugged her, as they flew together. He felt his heart open up even more when she told him that he was a good man, a good family man. He was also quite pleased to hear Grandma tell him that there weren't many adults like him who chose to remain open.

54

"It is a wonderful ability you have, Jim. To be open is to be childlike and adults think that this is wrong, but you don't think that way, Jim. It is important to tell Sue about the moths. Moths are signs for winning money. You must also remember that the electrician went to 24 Oxford Street near a park, where Molly is. The electrician will be next door to your house tomorrow morning. His name is Rob. Remember all these things, as they are important."

Grandma then floated out into the cool night air from the bedroom window, where she had just landed with Jim, then disappeared into the night, peaceful and wonderfully content. She knew that everyone she loved was also at peace, and enjoying the most amazing sleep they'd had in ages.

Far away from the Pratt house, Molly was sleeping quite comfortably on her tree branch, surrounded by the dragonfly Faeries, who were sleeping on the tiny twigs.

Molly, on her branch, had watched with wide open eyes all the activity happening below her that evening. Dogs appeared from everywhere, some on leads with their masters while others walked freely and tore through the very same bushes where Molly had been hiding earlier. The dogs were sniffing the ground and looking for the right bush to pee on. Molly was thankful she was not still hiding there.

When darkness fell and the park became quiet, Molly spotted a red fox dashing by the bush and watched as he suddenly picked up her cat scent. He sniffed and looked about, then went into the bushes expecting to find something in there that was perhaps good to eat. Molly shivered a little, very relieved to be up the tree.

Two badgers came around for their nightly stroll, looking for food. They waddled slowly by with big bellies headed in the direction of the park's rubbish bins. One of the badgers stopped at the base of Molly's tree and stretched his husky body up the trunk, digging his sharp claws into the bark. He let out a strange, fierce cry to his partner which sent shivers down

Molly's spine. The two badgers then moved on. During all of this time Molly didn't move a muscle, but she no longer felt afraid, as she knew the dark well enough and that the Faeries were with her.

Molly heard the flapping sounds of wings near her branch and suddenly three black bats went whizzing by, almost touching the whiskers on her face. Usually Molly would chase bats, but she had no thoughts of doing that tonight. Molly watched them circle the tree for some time and listened to their shrill calls to each other, as they flew away on their nightly hunt for food.

Earlier on, two green grass snakes had slithered out from the hedges looking for somewhere safer to go, their black tongues flicking in and out.

And Mr. Woodpecker had hammered his iron-like beak against the oak tree where Molly was, having his bedtime snack, and he seemed quite content as he slept in a hollow on a branch just above Molly.

Molly's tummy growled with hunger as they night crept in. "I would like to have a snack from Vicky," she thought, and a wave of sadness overcame her for a moment and with that, her spirits began to sink.

But the Faeries whispered in her ear, "All will be well tomorrow, all will be well." And Molly again began purring, feeling again much easier.

During this time, Vicky was having her dream where she saw Molly sitting on the branch of the old oak tree. She talked to Molly and told her to sleep well and that she would be there tomorrow. The dream seemed so real that when Vicky awoke for a brief moment, she knew that her dream would come true. Grandma had told her where to look for Molly...in the oak tree in the park where she would find her safe and well. Vicky then rolled onto her tummy, falling into a deep sleep.

Molly was also dreaming as she dozed on her branch. Vicky was talking to her in her comfortable, soothing voice, as she lay on Vicky's legs in her and Dennis's bedroom. Molly, in her dream, saw the many flickering bright lights that Bounder was seeing at that very moment in the room, coming from the fireflies who were really Faeries.

CHAPTER SIX

A brand new morning

When morning arrived at the Pratt house, Vicky was the first to wake, leaping out of bed and rubbing the Angel and Faerie dust from her eyes and shouted out to Dennis who was still sound asleep.

"Wake up Dennis!" she yelled. "Get out of bed! I want to tell you all about my dreams while they're still in my head!" She jumped on her brother's bed, shaking him while Bounder, who had stayed in their room that morning, looked up at Vicky with wide open eyes.

Dennis woke up instantly, saying in a very excited voice,

"I had a dream I was at Grandma's eating cake! It was so real, I thought I was awake!" He put on his t-shirt and reached under the bed for his socks and shoes.

Vicky answered her brother, saying,

"I saw Grandma too! And Angels and Faeries. They were all telling me what to do!" She took her blouse and pulled it over her light blond hair. "Grandma told me Molly is alive and in the park, and that she slept last night on a tree branch in the dark!"

Dennis told Vicky,

"Grandma told me where Mum's red shoe is, and stories about her teddy when she was young. She said Mummy would first think you were only dreaming up everything about Molly, that it wasn't real. When you tell her about the Angels and

58

Faeries, she would think you were being silly. That's what she would first feel."

Vicky said thoughtfully,

"Grandma told me to tell Mummy these things. It will show her how hope and belief which will make her heart sing."

"You've had the same type of dreams as me!" Dennis yelled in excitement. He then pulled his sister's arm as he headed towards the door. "Let's go wake up Mummy and Dad and tell them about our dreams. I can't believe I saw Grandma! Wow!"

"Dad has gone to work early today," Vicky said. "We have to let Mummy wake up slowly before we tell her what Grandma had to say."

As they walked down the narrow hallway past their parent's room, Dennis said in a worried voice, "What if Mummy doesn't believe us at all?"

A shadow of doubt flashed upon Vicky's face. "We will then make up a story to go out, and go to the park alone."

"We will get into trouble for lying," Dennis said.

"We can't leave Molly on a branch hungry and dying," Vicky replied with determination in her voice.

"How do you know which park she's in?" Dennis asked.

"The electric man is coming next door and he will know," Vicky answered.

"How would he know?"

"Molly jumped into his van yesterday when he was working next door, and then he drove away to his next job with Molly hiding inside. That's where the park is and where the Angels told me I will find Molly."

Dennis shouted with glee. "I remember more about my dreams! I was talking with Maisy, Daisy and Duncan. Duncan is really smart and wise. I didn't think his brain was that big a size!"

They looked at each other and burst out laughing, while Bounder circled around Dennis's legs, drawn to their excited energy.

"Let's go visit the rabbits, Vicky!" Dennis said with excitement. "I want to tell Duncan I have hope in my heart and that is all I need for a start!"

Vicky and Dennis ran downstairs into the back garden, with Dennis this time very mindful of where he stepped, not wanting to crush the ants or dandelions or disturb any rocks, and carefully made their way to the rabbit hutch.

As a matter of fact, Dennis noticed a most peculiar rock sticking out along the garden path, and picking it up he gently rubbed his hand along its smoothness. He then spoke to it, saying, "I BELIEVE!"

Before going over to the rabbit hutches, Dennis thought of something important that he had to do, and walked down to the pond and stuck his hands into the water, pulling out the wise old rock he had thrown into the pond yesterday. He held the rock, caressing it, and placed it back in the exact same spot it had been yesterday. Then he rushed over to the rabbit hutch, excited to tell Duncan what he had just done.

Maisy, Daisy and Duncan seemed extremely pleased when they saw Vicki and Dennis, kicking their hind legs against the hutch with enthusiasm. As they did this, Dennis saw the tiny balls of light and Faerie dust began to fall on him, almost like it was snowing. He could see the Angels. "I BELIEVE!" Dennis shouted. "I BELIEVE!"

****

As we know, the Angels and Faeries and Grandma had visited Mother Pratt last night, but this morning when she awoke, she only remembered bits of her dreams. It was as if a cloud was blocking her memory and this made her feel very groggy, quite the opposite of how Vicky and Dennis were feeling.

You see, Vicky and Dennis were quite open to receiving the energy during the night from the Angels and the Faeries. Their hearts were more open and so they lit up much like a candle does when it lights up a dark room. Mother Pratt, on the other hand, was open in her dreams, but not so much when she was awake. Her open and hopeful energy from her dream-world was now being pushed away by the shadows of doubt which she had unknowingly built up inside of herself.

"Dreams are nothing but make-believe," Mother Pratt muttered, after remembering bits and pieces that didn't make much sense to her.

She was feeling very confused. Part of her knew that her mother (Grandma) had come into her dreams last night, giving messages that were important for her remember. But the other half of her was saying, "Forget about it. It was only a dream."

However, Mother Pratt could still hear her mother's gentle voice, and she began to remember more of her dream, which can happen after we wake up. However, at other times, we can forget everything about our dreams, but Mother Pratt's dream was too powerful to forget.

"You have to relax more, Sue," Grandma had said to her. "You are far too busy in your mind and being that busy is not helping you feel happy. I know you miss me a lot, but I want you to know that I'm happy where I am. I'm with your father and with many of my friends who have left the Earth. You know, Sue, when I died, I only moved on to where another world is, where we will all meet up again, so please enjoy your life down on earth, with all who you meet and all that you do. Enjoy Dennis and Vicky. They are brilliant children who are open to the energy they receive, as you once were when you were a child.

"Have fun with Vicky and Dennis as they grow up, and remember, they know of things that you do not. Remember that, Sue. The children know. They KNOW. Always listen to them with an open heart as if you were still a child yourself, because the children believe in us and they trust us. We learn from everyone, and I know you know this in your heart. Have fun and be more childlike sweetheart. Be more childlike."

****

Mother Pratt was trying to remember more about her dream and what her mother had to say to her but her mind was forgetting, and she began to once again feel sad, when Vicky and Dennis came running into the kitchen. They found Mother Pratt deep in thought as she sat at the table, her hands cupped around a steaming mug of tea.

They had much to tell and both excitedly spoke at once, until Mother Pratt finally held up her hand and said, "One at a time, please!"

Vicky began to speak first about the events of her dreams, but Mother Pratt didn't want to hear what she was saying.

"Nonsense!" Mother Pratt said, as she couldn't believe Vicky knew where Molly was and that it was Grandma who had told her where to find her. It was just impossible!

Dennis grabbed a piece of cold toast from the table, and as he spread some jam on it, said in a very important voice, "I know your missing red shoe is under the bureau by your bed. Grandma told me last night. She also told me that your favourite watch, the one that was broken is working again. The watch is tucked inside your red sweater in your second bureau drawer."

But Mother Pratt didn't go and look, as Vicky and Dennis had hoped, so that she could have her proof, as Grandma had said. Instead, she busied herself clearing away the dishes from the table. In her groggy mind, she had forgotten to make fresh toast for Vicky and Dennis. She then said to them,

"I don't want to hear any more about dreams right now. I know you are both upset about Molly. I am as well, but you must understand that Molly could be anywhere, in any park, if she is in fact in a park. How could you possibly know where the park is?" Mother Pratt silenced any replies by holding her hand up for them not to speak.

"Let me finish my tea in a bit of peace, please!" she said. "Then I must go to the shop down the street. When I return we will look for Molly again. We shall go around all the houses on our street. It's the best we can do. We can't be looking on every single street and in every park."

Vicky protested. "We do know which park Molly is in, mother! Grandma showed me where. Why won't you believe me? Don't you care?"

Mother Pratt became silent. Vicky's face had such a look of certainty that it was difficult for her to completely ignore what she was saying. 'How could this be true?' Mother Sue thought to herself. 'Did my mother really come into all our dreams. Is it possible?'

Dennis scooted upstairs into his mother and father's room and looked under the bureau, and sure enough there was the red shoe. Next, Dennis opened the second drawer of his mother's bureau and found the red sweater. He pulled out his mother's favourite watch which was steadily ticking. It was working! He let out a whoop of joy and ran downstairs with the watch and both of her red shoes clutched in his hands to proudly show his mom.

"Look!" Dennis yelled excitedly, showing Mother Sue her shoes and watch. "It's true! It's true! I knew I was right. Grandma did come last night!"

"Look!" Dennis yelled excitedly

Mother Pratt's mouth opened wide and her eyes indeed looked shocked, but no words came out. She ran upstairs to look for her watch, not believing that the watch Dennis had shown her was really her own. Adults can be so stubborn at times! Mother Pratt looked through her drawer several times, pulling her clothes out as she looked for her watch, but of course there was no other watch. Dennis most certainly had it in his hand and it was working! Mother Pratt felt angry because she was very confused but her mind, which wanted proof, was still being stubborn, refusing to admit that she, Vicky and Dennis had really talked with Grandma in their dreams.

"It's just not possible," Mother Pratt said to herself again. "After all, Angels and Faeries are only stories for children, not adults! And as for Grandma giving us all messages and telling Vicky and Dennis that she knows where Molly is, well I just can't believe it."

Mother Sue went back downstairs and became Mother Pratt again as she scolded Vicky and Dennis.

"You had no right going into my bureau drawer, Dennis, no right at all!" Then she said to Vicky, "Who fixed my watch? Did you? The jeweler told me it could never be fixed."

"The Angels in our dreams fixed your watch, Mummy," Vicky replied. "It was Grandma and the Angels who told me where to find Molly. Why don't you believe us?"

"Because these things just don't happen, Vicky. Dreams are not real and neither are Angels that come to visit you in the night. You are picking up parts of stories read in fairy tale books."

"But what about your shoes and your watch that was broken? And what about me knowing how you found your teddy bear in the rubbish bin?" Dennis asked Mother Pratt. "Grandma told me last night you shared all your secrets with him."

Mother Pratt gasped in surprise at what Dennis had said.

How could he know? She left the dirty dishes in the sink to go upstairs to her room to get a light jacket because the day was cloudy and cool. "I need time to think," she thought. "Time to think."

The truth was that Mother Sue was about to cry, which was why she couldn't continue speaking with Vicky and Dennis, or especially to reply to what Dennis had just told her about her teddy. Again, it was impossible that he could know anything about Teddy. Impossible!

Mother Sue didn't want Vicky and Dennis to see her in this state. She wondered about Grandma telling Vicky where Molly was. It was all too much for her busy mind. She felt ready to explode. It was all too much for her to believe. She needed time by herself.

She entered her bedroom and closed the door. "How could Dennis know about Teddy?" she asked herself again. "I had Teddy when I was a little girl!" Tears ran down her face, as thinking of Teddy made her realize she missed talking to him. She certainly missed her mother (Grandma) and at that moment, she knew she missed herself, the Sue who was at one time a little girl.

Mother Sue took Teddy out of a box hidden in her wardrobe and sat on the bed hugging him in a very loving way as she cried a little more. It had been a long time since Teddy was out of his box, and he felt Mother Sue's energy of love because he was energy as well, and he had missed the little girl who had grown up to become Vicky and Dennis's mother, who had turned into Mother Pratt. Teddy had felt terribly alone sitting in the box in the dark wardrobe, left there for so many years. He wanted to cry as well, but because he didn't know how, he just simply became the energy of love which Mother Sue always had for him and that was enough for Teddy. He had been waiting such a long time.

****

65

Meanwhile, at work, Father Jim was feeling quite happy as he thought about his dreams last night. He was also a little confused, wondering if everything that he'd seen in his dreams was actually real. 'How could that be?' he asked himself. He was also worried about Molly. The situation didn't appear to be good. "I hope it changes today and some miracle brings our Molly back," he said out loud.

Grandma had told him he was a good man who had an open heart. He had a childlike energy, Grandma had said, and this is what adults should never lose.

Father Jim had always felt this, but his message from Grandma had pleased him even more because he knew now that it was not silly to be silly. Memories of his dreams became more clear, just like a curtain opening in a dark room, when suddenly the bright rays of sunlight pour in.

He recalled Grandma saying that the electrician was at 24 Oxford Street. He wrote the address down, for as we know, Father Jim was used to writing notes to himself. Then he suddenly remembered that Grandma had said this information would be important, and a name flashed into his memory, Rob.

"Yes," he said out loud. "That's the name...Rob" Grandma had said, 'Remember 24 Oxford Street, and behind the flats, there is a park!' "How odd!"

Father Jim wrote the name Rob on the scrap of paper and placed it in his shirt pocket.

It all seemed to make sense in his dream, but he was now left wondering what the messages were all about. And why did Grandma say that moths bring money? Jim sat a long while at his desk with his work papers in front of him, but he was not reading them. He knew there were more details in his dreams from last night, but was now having difficulty remembering all of them. He said to himself, "I will have to speak to Sue about this when I get home later today, and see if any of this makes sense to her."

****

Mother Pratt had composed herself and walked downstairs to the front door, buttoning up her coat. Vicky was disappointed. She had hoped her Mother would have said something like, "Let's all go the park to find Molly, children," or "Tell me more about what Grandma said to you." But all she said was, "We will talk about everything when I return. I promise, love. Right now I need to go out and think, and going to the shop will help me. I promise I won't be long."

When the front door closed behind her mother, Vicky went to look out the living room window, watching her mother walk down the busy street. Mother Pratt didn't notice a dark blue van pulling up to the house next door. Had she just once looked back, she would have seen Vicky run out and if she had returned to listen, she would have learned quite a bit more that would have made her believe.

Vicky knew this was the van. It had words written on the side saying Electrical Division R.D.

"The electrical man is next door, Dennis" Vicky shouted out excitably. "Come on! Let's catch him before he goes into the house."

There was no cause to worry about that, though. The electrician was taking his time looking through his tool case as Vicky ran out to him, with Dennis right behind her. She began to tell him her story. However, Vicky changed it a little bit. She thought to tell a white lie so the electrician would believe. She said that a neighbour walking on the street had actually seen her cat, Molly, jump inside the back of the van. Vicky thought that was a better way rather then say that her Grandma with the Angels and Faeries had shown her this in a dream. Dennis kept quiet, deciding it was best to let Vicky tell the story, especially since he didn't know what story she was going to tell.

"It's quite surprising that I took your cat to my next job without me noticing or hearing her," the electrician said. He took out his workbook with the list of his service calls from the previous day and said, "Of course, having the address is a good start, but what makes you think you can find your cat there? I don't want to disappoint you, luv, but it is a big area to search for her, you know."

"I was told to look for her in the park. I'm sure she went there after dark." Vicky immediately covered her mouth with her hands, realizing that the electrician would ask her how she knew about the park. But it was too late to cover up her mistake.

"Park?" the electrician asked with curiosity in his voice. "Right! There is a park nearby. Tell me, luv, how would you know about that if you don't know the area?" His eyes looked a little nervous.

"I don't know," Vicky answered. "I just thought there would be one, and that's where my cat would go."

"Well, that's one spot of good luck for your cat that she has a smart girl like yourself as her owner," the electrician smiled at Vicky. He had curly brown hair that stuck out from under his company cap, and a busy beard to match. Vicky liked him.

The electrician offered to give her and Dennis a lift, provided their parents agreed, but it would have to be after his job was done in two or three hours. Vicky knew this was too long a wait.

"Thank you very much," Vicky replied. "But Dennis and I will walk to the park, as I feel there is no time to waste, so we must make haste. Did you say it was only two miles?"

"A little less than that, luv. No more than an hour's walk." The electrician tucked his shirt into his trousers, showing a fair sized belly. He tipped his cap to Vicky and Dennis, wishing them good luck on their journey. "I really hope you find your cat. I'm sorry I didn't notice her." He was about to walk up the steps when he stopped and said, "Excuse me, luv, but what makes you think your cat jumped out at my next stop and not any of the others? After all, I only had the back doors open for a short time."

"Oh, the Angels told me!" Vicky said without thinking. "Err, I

68

mean um..."

The electrician smiled at Vicky. "That's okay, luv. If the Angels told you, then I believe you. You seem to know everything else, why not that?" The electrician tugged gently on his beard and said, "I'd like the Angels to come and tell me a thing or two." Then he picked up his toolbox again and walked up the steps to the house, whistling one of the tunes he always whistled when he was on the job.

Talking with Vicky had brightened up his day. He was feeling more cheerful and happy. This is what good energy does. It passes from one person to another if they are open to receive it.

"Excuse me, sir!" Vicky yelled to the electrician just before he walked into the house. "I want to thank you very, very much! Could I ask what your name is?"

"Sure, luv. My name is Robert, but my friends call me Rob."

Vicky was ecstatic! That was the name Grandma had given to her last night. Again she had more proof!

"My name is Victoria!" she yelled back. "But everyone calls me Vicky."

"And I'm Dennis!" Dennis cried out, as he had not said a word up until then.

"Pleased to meet you, Vicky," Rob said, as he rang the bell and opened the door of the house. "And you too, Dennis. I was wondering if the cat had got your tongue, but I know now that isn't the case!"

Rob the electric man, paused on the doorstep and called out,

"Hold on a sec, luv, let me write some simple directions for you. He pulled a pen from his back pocket and began to scribble directions on a small scrap of paper found in another pocket.

"He's just like dad!" Dennis said to Vicky and they both laughed.

Vicky ran back into the house with Dennis, as now they

were on a mission, an adventure, on their way to rescue Molly. When they walked into the house, they noticed Bounder had been watching everything from the window ledge. Pretty Boy was sitting in his cage, saying in his budgie voice, "Look at the birdies! Look at the birdies!"

CHAPTER SEVEN

An adventure of their own

Dennis had taken Maisy, Daisy and Duncan out of their hutches earlier on, so now he went to the garden to put them back in before he and Vicky began their journey. The day was very gloomy. Dark clouds had once again gathered overnight and this time it seemed certain that it would rain. Dennis was sending his thoughts towards Duncan, wondering if Duncan could really hear his words, or whether he saw pictures of his thoughts.

"It looks like it's going to pour buckets of rain today," Vicky said to Dennis. "Let's go rescue Molly before the rain is here to stay."

Dennis jumped to his feet, placing the rabbits back into their hutches and said aloud, "Wish us luck Maisy, Daisy and Duncan."

The rabbits twitched their noses and thumped their strong back feet on their hutches, seemingly answering Dennis.

Vicky left a note for Mother, saying they were going to find Molly and that she shouldn't worry. 'I am going to be in BIG trouble!' she thought. 'But I have no choice. I have to believe what Grandma and the Angels told me last night. Mother isn't ready to listen yet, and the time to go is now before the rain comes.'

Vicky and Dennis went out the front door, telling Bounder

that they would be back soon with Molly. Vicky was carrying Molly's cat cage with one hand and holding Dennis's hand with the other. Dennis tried to break free of his sister's hand.

"I'm old enough to walk without holding your hand, Vicky. Let me go! Your hand feels wet and sticky."

"You will hold my hand on this street, Dennis," Vicky replied in a firm voice, as the busy traffic buzzed by them. "You can be a big help though, if you carry the cage." This pleased Dennis as he felt in charge and strong.

. "You can be a big help though, if you carry the cage."

They stopped once for Vicky to look at the paper Rob the electrician had given her with directions on how to get to Oxford Street. It was rather simple, a right turn at the top of their road, continue straight for almost a mile, and then another right turn at Oxford Street where the crossroad was. The electrician even wrote that this was a busy crossroad, and to be careful there and nearby the house, 24 Oxford Street, there was a lane leading to the park.

He had also told Vicky to ask directions from people if she wasn't certain of where they were going. Because she was looking at directions and making sure Dennis was safely by her side, she didn't notice that the dragonfly Faeries were right beside them. But Dennis did.

"Vicky! Look! The dragonflies are following us!" Vicky looked above her head and saw the dragonflies whizzing around them, almost as if they were leading the way and in fact they were. They were guiding them.

"Wow!" Vicky said in amazement. "I believe the dragonflies are showing us the way to the park, Dennis! And I believe those dragonflies are the Faeries we saw last night in the dark!"

When they reached the first traffic lights, Vicky paused, uncertain for a moment if they were to turn left or right. She was just about to once again take out the electrical man's paper from her pocket when Dennis blurted out, "Look, Vicky! The dragonflies are turning right. Come on! Let's follow them! We have a green light!"

So they followed the dragonflies halfway down the street, where Vicky stopped a man passing by and asked directions, just to be sure.

The man told Vicky, "Carry on straight, luv, you are going in the right direction. When you come to the big crossroads, you have reached Oxford Street."

The dragonflies floated around his head as he spoke, and the man said, "Blimey, what on Earth are those things doing on the street? Quite an annoyance!" He swatted his arms around his head, looking a little bit afraid, and moved on rather quickly forgetting all about Vicky and Dennis.

Dennis said to his sister as they continued down the road, "If only the grown-ups could see what we see. I think everyone would be a lot happier!"

Vicky agreed. "Imagine telling that man that the dragonflies are leading us and I was just double-checking with him. He would have thought that we were crazy and told us to be on our way!"

Dennis said, laughing, "I think he went on his way, all right! That man almost started to run, afraid that the dragonflies were going to bite his bum!" Vicky laughed with him.

****

Father Jim was just about to call home and tell Sue the great luck which had just happened, when the phone rang and there she was on the line, her voice in a panic.

She was talking extremely fast, telling Jim that Vicky and Dennis had left the house on their own.

"To go to some park to look for Molly! She said Grandma had told them where Molly was in their dreams! Can you imagine, Jim?" Sue asked doubtfully.

Mother Sue continued to talk, giving Jim so much information and detail about Vicky and Dennis's dreams and even snippets of her own dreams that his head became dizzy. Her voice was nervous and excited.

"Dennis knew where my missing shoe was and you know my watch, Jim, the one you gave me for Christmas years ago? The one that doesn't work any longer? Well, it does now! And Dennis knew that it was working and which drawer it was wrapped up in."

Jim held the phone a little away from his ear, not meaning to be disrespectful to Sue; he wanted to listen and help but the energy passing from her was nervous energy and he needed to keep calm.

"The children told me, Jim, that it was my mother who came to them in their dreams! I didn't want to believe them, but I have to admit, I also had dreams of my mother last night." Sue's voice began to tremble over the phone and Jim knew this was too much for her to handle.

"Now, Sue! I'm asking you to calm down for a moment and pay attention to what I have to say. Are you okay to listen?" Jim heard a weak yes in reply and then he said. "Last night I too had dreams of your mother." There was silence on the other end of the phone, so Jim continued. "Sue, is there a van parked outside the house by any chance?"

"Yes, yes there is," Sue answered. "How on Earth would you know that, Jim?"

"And is it an electrician's truck?" Jim asked again.

"Why yes, it is, Jim! How do you know this?" Sue asked, a bit frightened. "Why are you asking about this van?"

"Because I believe that your mother's messages are true. They are quite real." There was a silence over the phone. Jim continued in an excited voice, which wasn't usual for him, "Last night Sue, Grandma told me that moths bring money and that you had found moths in the closet the other day and didn't care for that. She said you were going to kill them with a broom, but Vicky and Dennis prevented that and took them outside. Well, just five minutes ago I checked our lottery tickets and we have won five thousand pounds! Imagine that, Sue! Five thousand pounds!"

Sue was shocked and stunned into silence.

Jim went on, "Grandma told me that moths bring money and she also told me that Rob, the electrician next door, knows which park it is that Vicky and Dennis went to. In fact, Grandma told me the address is 24 Oxford Street and if we were to go to the park nearby, that's where we will find Molly." Jim paused but there was still no response. "Hello, Sue, are you still there?"

Sue answered very quickly. "Yes, I am Jim. I'm not sure I understand anything anymore. I only want to find Vicky and Dennis." Her voice sounded lighter. Jim could hear the change and felt that he could see her face lighting up almost into a smile, and he knew something had gotten through to her. It was belief, of course.

"I can't believe we have won five thousand pounds!" Sue finally said, her voice full of wonder. "And Mother had told me those exact things, Jim, about moths and money. I thought it was all just some silly dream."

Incredible as it all sounded to Sue's ears, she had to admit to herself that much of what occurred while everyone was sleeping was indeed true! "Oh lord! I can't believe it!" Sue said with a burst of excitement, as a big opening exploded into her heart. Sue really believed this time. She really did believe!

"Now, let's go find Vicky and Dennis," Father Jim said to Mother Sue. "I shall leave work and go straight to that address, 24 Oxford Street, and look for that park. Why don't you go next door and have a word with the electrician and give me a ring back when you see what he has to say. I will wait for you call before I leave, alright luv?"

Mother Sue agreed and they said their good-byes for the moment.

****

Morning found Molly still sitting on the branch of the old tree. She was extremely thirsty and quite hungry, for it had been twenty-four hours since she had eaten. She had thought of trying to climb down the tree, which she was definitely not good at doing. She was forgetting what the Faeries had told her last night, that help was coming and Vicky would arrive today.

The main thing that kept Molly from climbing down was all the busy activity beneath her. It had started early in the morning when the workmen for the park first came with their cutting machines and went directly to the hedge where Molly had been hiding. They used a noisy electric cutter, which made Molly shake with fear.

If Molly had remained in those hedges, she would have had a fox sniff her out and try to kill her for food. Then goodness knows what the badgers would have done if they had found her. And now, the noisy park workers would have chased her out into the openness of the park! Her tummy rumbled again and her mouth was so dry.

Once the workers left, other human adults came, some on their way to work while others were walking their dogs. Still more humans were reading pieces of paper (newspaper), as they sat on the grass and on the benches. It seemed to Molly that many of them were talking loudly to themselves, while holding on to their ears, which puzzled her. Of course Molly couldn't know that they were using mobile phones.

The dark, cloudy summer morning still brought children of all ages (who were now free from school) out to the park, and they were playing all sorts of games with each other. Most of the children had happy energy inside of them, as they laughed with each other and yelled with joy. But there were some other children who were not so happy inside. They had forgotten about good, positive energy.

These were the ones who looked for trouble, as some of them were bullies. Having less hope in their heart gave them less things to believe in that were good.

Unfortunately for Molly, she was spotted up in the tree by one of the boys, one who was looking for trouble. A group of these boys immediately decided to have a contest to see who could hit the cat with a rock. They didn't seem to care that the rocks might injure or perhaps even kill her. They were only interested in the challenge of proving whose aim was the best of all.

A rock zipped by Molly's head and another hit the branch she was sitting on, ruffling the leaves around her. That was close enough for Molly, and she scurried further up the tree, halfway to the top. They threw more rocks, but Molly was now further away and thankfully the stones fell short of their mark. The boys began looking for smaller stones that could be thrown farther.

Then all of a sudden, the dragonflies who were Faeries surrounded the boys, darting around their heads, distracting them for the moment at least from throwing more rocks. They began flicking their hands wildly around, trying to swat the dragonflies. One boy though, who was bolder than his mates, the leader of the gang, ignored the dragonflies and picked up a perfectly-sized stone. As he stretched back to throw it at Molly, a girl screamed at him in a high-pitched voice. Vicky and Dennis had arrived just in time.

"Stop that!" Vicky yelled. "Stop throwing those rocks! That's my cat up there in that tree! Don't you dare hurt Molly!" She ran to the boy's side and tore the rock from his hand.

The boy looked at her with a snarl and said, "What do you mean that's your cat in the tree? Why should that stop me from chucking this rock at her?" The other boys laughed, which encouraged the bully to carry on. "I can throw this rock at you instead, if you'd like."

Dennis said very bravely, "You'll be sorry if you don't leave my sister alone. You'd better just move on and go home!"

The bully looked at Dennis with mean eyes, as Dennis was much smaller and younger than these boys.

"Sorry, mate?" the bully questioned Dennis. "Did you say we'll be sorry?" He laughed. "What do you think you can do about it, you skinny, twit?" He walked towards Dennis, staring him down and looking quite ready to push him around.

Dennis, normally would have been afraid, perhaps feeling to run away, or worse, even start to cry, but not today - not today. He felt determined that these bullies wouldn't block them, after all he and Vicky, and certainly Molly, had gone through. He just knew somehow that he was going to find a way out of this predicament and that the Angels would help him.

Vicky ran over to the oak tree, calling up to Molly to reassure her, to let her know that she was here. "Molly! It's okay. I'm here now!"

Molly recognized Vicky's voice and let out a weak, "Meow." She was trembling with fear after having rocks thrown at her, and some part of her questioned whether this was really Vicky, as cats have different ways of seeing and recognizing who we are.

The bully, roughly pushed Dennis away and picked up another rock, a bigger one this time, and was aiming it at Molly while the other boys watched with amusement and cheered him on. Some of them picked up more rocks to throw.

Dennis shouted, "Angels, stop him! Stop them! Stop their arms!"

A very odd thing then happened to those boys, something they would never forget. Hundreds of dragonflies surrounded them, circling around their heads like a swarm of bees. The bully tried to throw his rock, more determined than ever, but couldn't lift his arm higher than his shoulder as the big stone in his hand suddenly became much too heavy to hold, and he had no choice but to let it fall to the ground.

"I can't lift my arm," one boy said in panic.

"Neither can I!" said another.

"It's him," said the bully, pointing at Dennis. "Somehow, he's put a spell on us. He's done some magic on us! I heard him say, 'Angels, make them stop!'"

Dennis said with a strong voice, "Now go away, you've had your fun. Go now while you still have a chance to run!" He pointed his finger at the bully's legs, just as a dragonfly bit his nose. The bully yelled with shock and fear, wondering if Dennis could really do something to his legs. He quickly dashed away with the other boys following close behind!

They ran as if their lives depended on it, and Dennis laughed at the events that had just happened. The Angels have rules to not interfere, but in this case they were called to help and quite strongly by Dennis, and so when this happens, the Angels can stretch the rules a little bit!

Dennis ran over to the tree that Vicky was trying to climb. The lower branch was too high for her to grab onto. "What are we to do?" she asked Dennis with surprise on her face, after witnessing what had happened with the bullies and what he had done.

Molly was looking down at Vicky with her big green eyes and began to meow at her, for she was now certain it was Vicky below the tree. The energy of fear left her when the boys ran away, changing into the energy of hope. Molly was no longer frightened, but was tired and hungry and wanted desperately to come down and go home with Vicky.

Dennis said to Vicky, "The Angels will help us about what to do, just as they did with those boys. Did you see what happened to them, Vicky?"

Before Vicky could answer, a young man in jogging pants and hooded sweatshirt came by where the children were standing and asked if they needed some help.

"Is that your cat up there in the tree?" he asked.

"Yes, it is," Vicky replied. "I can't reach the branch to climb up and get her. I'm not sure what to do next."

"Hmm," the young man said, thinking out loud. "I think I can climb up that old oak tree, but will your cat scratch me if I try to pick her up?"

" No, she won't," Vicky answered with hope entering her voice. "Molly has been stuck in trees before and it does seem more often lately, but she has always allowed strangers to help her out. You just need to be gentle with her when you get close. You can stroke her head. She likes that and then she will trust you."

"Okay then," the young man said to Vicky with confidence in his voice. "I shall attempt to take a hike up that tree. Also, I have a blanket where me girlfriend is. I'll go and fetch it. That way I can drop your Molly onto the blanket when I need to jump off that last branch to get down. You and your brother can hold the blanket the way fireman do. That sound alright, mates?"

Vicky and Dennis nodded their approval.

"The funny thing is," the young man continued. "I don't remember deciding to walk this way. I was going to the loo, you know, which happens to be in the other direction. It was like someone was moving my legs to come this way instead. Really, it's the oddest thing."

The young man gazed up towards the top branches of the oak where Molly was, growing more impatient now and meowing more. However, the young man continued to talk.

"It was like I was guided here, because I certainly didn't feel like walking the long way to the loo. You know, when one has to go, one has to go!" Dennis's eyes opened wide, nodding in agreement, having been in that situation several times before.

"The Angels were guiding you," Dennis said very seriously.

"You know what, my little mate, you and my girlfriend are going to hit it off very well! She talks like that, speaking about Angels and energy and such things. I think, more and more, I'm beginning to believe in all those things myself."

The young man looked up the tree again, and saw dozens of dragonflies floating up towards Molly, landing right beside her. He couldn't possibly know that they were speaking to her with their thoughts.

The Faeries were saying, "Help is here Molly! Vicky is here and she is coming to rescue you. You are going home soon."

The young man, who had his dark hair tied into a ponytail, stared at the dragonflies and said, "Very interesting all of this, very interesting indeed. I believe I ran into some young lads on my way here, even though I wasn't really on my way here, and they were running from dragonflies, or so I thought I heard them say. One lad was yelling about dragonflies biting him and something about a lad who knew something about magic. Hmm, all too interesting, I'd say." He looked straight at Dennis for a time, then smiled and said, "Right, you two! Just wait here and I shall return in a few minutes with my girlfriend and our blanket, but first I shall dash to the loo because right now it is rather urgent, if you beg my pardon."

The young man returned with his pretty girlfriend in no time at all. 'He really must have flown,' Dennis thought. 'Just like the dragonflies.'

The man climbed up onto the branch that had been too high for Vicky and continued climbing up the other branches, which were long and thick and easy to hold onto. As he came towards Molly, her cat instinct made her move backwards on the branch. However, the young man was calm and gently put his hand out towards Molly while speaking to her. She was able to sniff the goodness of energy that came from him and she relaxed, allowing him to stroke her head for a few moments.

Molly kept hearing Vicky's voice which helped her to stay calm. The young man carefully picked Molly up, holding her close to his chest and she felt his protective energy and knew she was safe to take the journey down with him. The young man carefully climbed back down the thick branches of the old oak tree.

When he reached the last limb, he yelled down to Vicky, Dennis and his girlfriend to stretch out the blanket so he could drop Molly into it. They shouted back that they were ready and to let Molly go, and as she dropped into the blanket, she felt that she was flying like in a dream.

Then, in a flash, she was in Vicky's arms being hugged and smothered with kisses.

The young man jumped to the ground from the branch and was met by his girlfriend, who also gave him hugs and kisses for a job well done.

It was at that very moment that Mother Sue and Father Jim arrived with Rob, the electrician

Molly felt that she was flying like in a dream.

Test of faith

"Vicky!" Mother Sue called to her. "Oh, Vicky, you have Molly! You knew all along. You knew!" Mother Sue was so relieved and happy. She hugged Vicky, squashing Molly just a little as she kissed Vicky, while rubbing Molly's soft, furry head.

Vicky was overjoyed to see her parents with the electrician in tow.

"Mum! Dad! You found us just in time and I think all because of Rob!" she said excitedly.

"Hello, luv," said Rob. "We meet again, and under much better circumstances, I see."

Father Jim explained, as he always liked to do, for he loved telling stories.

"Rob brought your mother in his van and I came directly from work, so we met outside the park."

"But how did you know to talk with the electric man, er, I mean Rob," Vicky asked, puzzled.

"I didn't know exactly," Father Jim replied. "The truth is, I had a dream last night of Grandma and in the dream I was advised to look for a certain number on Oxford Street. Number 24 was the message. I was also advised by Grandma to talk with Rob, who we are calling the electric man." Father Jim turned to Rob and said, "I apologize for still calling you the electric man now that we know your name, but we will continue to do so only for explaining these extraordinary circumstances."

Rob laughed away and said, "That's just fine, Jim. I don't mind at all. The electric man has a nice ring to it. I believe I will paint that name onto my van. 'Rob the Electric Man,' or maybe I shall just write 'The Electric Man can save your day!'"

"So, to shorten this story for now, Vicky (as Father Jim was certainly going to tell this story for a long time), your mother was very worried when she read your note that you were going to some park to look for Molly. I knew this was very odd business because Grandma had told me about a park near number 24 Oxford Street. Fancy that! Then your mother saw Rob's van when she returned from the shops and after speaking with me, went next door to have a word with him. That was my advice! I said, Sue, we have to get to the bottom of this. Go and have a word with the electrical man and call me straight back."

Father Jim would have carried on with the story, but Mother Sue felt it was time to have a chat with the other people, who had helped rescue Molly. She said to the young man and his girlfriend,

"I want to thank you so much for your help. We greatly appreciate what you have done." Mother Sue held out her hand and said, "May I ask your names?"

"I'm Jimmy and this is Susie," the young man answered.

"That's the name of our Mum and Dad!" Dennis said, with surprise in his voice.

"How about that!" both Jims said together.

"How can we ever repay you? Mother Sue asked.

"Please, please, Sue!" Jimmy replied. "It was my pleasure to help out, indeed it was. In fact, I think I was brought here to help by invisible forces. Aye, that I do think, but that's a story for another day."

"I know how we can repay them!" Vicky shouted with excitement. "We can have a party, a barbecue in the back garden and invite everyone here. We can do it this weekend."

"That would be fine," Mother Sue happily said. "We could do a barbecue, couldn't we, Jim?"

"Yes, by all means we can," Father Jim replied, already beginning to daydream. He had been staring up at the huge gathering of dragonflies who were still lingering around the branches of the oak tree.

"Would you please come?" Vicky asked her new friends.

"Well, yes, we would certainly be happy to come," Jimmy

answered while looking at his girlfriend for agreement.

Susie smiled and said, "Jimmy and I would love to come, but you should know, we are vegetarians. We haven't eaten animals for several years now, so we hope that won't bother you."

"Well," said Father Jim. "As a matter of fact, I was reading some articles just the other day about more people becoming vegetarians and I found it most interesting. I would like to look into that a bit more, so perhaps you could explain more to me what types of dishes vegetarians cook. I would like to make notes on this. As for the barbecue, we can make it a vegetarian barbecue, if that is possible.

"We shall bring some very tasty vegetarian food that you can barbecue. It will be our pleasure," Susie said.

"Well, we can all pitch in together," Mother Sue said. "After all, you are to be our guests. I shall make different salads and bake some deserts."

"Do you like rabbits?" Vicky asked the young couple.

"Uh, yes, we do like rabbits," Susie answered, a little worried that the barbecue may have something to do with cooking rabbits.

"Why do you ask?"

"Because we have three rabbits, and Maisy is about to have babies."

Mother Sue laughed, "I think Vicky is thinking of homes for the babies."

"Oh...ah!" young Jimmy said. "That sounds interesting, but we will need to have a think about that as we are often away."

Molly was beginning to meow and wriggle against Vicky's arms, and Vicky said over everybody's excited voices, "Molly has had enough. She's hungry and thirsty. I think we should go now if that's okay."

"Yes, yes, let's go!" Father Jim said, looking around for anything that might be left behind while checking his pockets for a business card, as well as his car keys. He then said to the young couple, "Come to our house this Saturday around four o'clock and we will have a bit of a party in the back garden."

The young couple nodded as Father Jim handed over a business card with their address on it.

Vicky, still struggling with Molly, asked Rob the electrical man to come to their party as well.

Rob seemed pleased by the invitation. "Yes, Vicky, luv. I would really like to come, and I will bring my missus with me, as I have a missus you know, as well as a young daughter. Perhaps we will take a look at one of those baby rabbits."

"They haven't been born yet," Dennis said, laughing beside him as they began to walk away from the oak tree and the hedge that Molly went into when she frantically first entered the park. "But it should be any day now, and who knows, maybe it's happened today. Everything else has!"

Mother Sue told Rob that he and his family would be most honoured guests at their barbecue.

****

Molly was in Vicky's arms being hugged.

They said goodbye to the young couple and the Pratt family, with Rob the electrical man and of course Molly, who was now in her cage, all walked down the very same lane that Molly had run through to get to the park. The same pit bull dog was tied up, asleep on the grass beside his house. The difference today was he didn't bark or race towards anyone. The energy surrounding the travelers was peaceful, calm and happy. The pit bull opened his sleepy eyes at the passers-by, then fell back to sleep, just like he was drugged. This was the first time that this had ever happened, people passing by the dog without him madly barking at them.

They crossed Oxford Street which was still busy with traffic and Father Jim, Mother Pratt, Vicky, Dennis and of course Molly got into their car, while Rob jumped into his van. He drove out first and waved to the Pratt family, whistling away. He felt happy and content knowing that he had helped a family out of a jam, even if most of it was done while they were all asleep!

The Pratt family were in a wonderful mood as they drove back home. Molly was safe and sound with them, they had met new friends and most especially the light of hope was back in the heart and soul of their family, particularly with Mother Pratt, who was going to be more like a Mother Sue now.

Mother Sue kept saying over and over to Vicky and Dennis that she believed everything they had been trying to tell her about their dreams about Grandma, and that she would never doubt them again. She said she had learned a very big lesson today and although she was a little cross at them for going to the park on their own, she certainly understood why.

"I am so relieved you children were not hurt and that Molly is safe," she said, turning to the back seat and scratching Molly on her head. Vicky had opened the cage door and gently pulled Molly onto her lap. Molly was now curled up into the crook of Vicky's arm, her eyes closed with a contented purr coming from her throat. She was happy and safe, back with her family and her very best friend.

Molly barely noticed the movement of the car, as usually she didn't like the car at all, but then again, that hadn't stopped her from jumping into the van. But that she wouldn't do again, she was thinking, (if cats really think that way), and then Molly thought again, 'Well, maybe if there was a little crack to peek into, then I could take just a little look, but I wouldn't ever, ever go into a place I didn't know. Well, I think I wouldn't....' And then she fell to sleep, taking one well-deserved cat nap.

"I'm so happy to have my family together," Mother Sue said, caressing the back of Father Jim's head as he drove. The new, happy energy was opening her up to the love and belief that had been asleep inside of her, but really, it wasn't ever that far away. It was only forgotten.

When they arrived at their house and pushed open the rusty car doors, the Pratt family, with Molly in tow, went into the back garden and met Bounder, who ran to greet Molly, his companion and sister, sniffing her strange park smells as they touched noses.

Vicky brought out some water and cat food, and after having a good drink, Molly only took a morsel of food (just as cats will often do) before going to visit Maisy, Daisy and Duncan to share her adventure with them.

She took a little while licking herself (as cats will often do), but the rabbits and Bounder waited patiently. Then she stretched her body, shaking the stiffness out of it, from all the hours sitting on the tree branch, then suddenly dashed around the yard with Bounder in pursuit. They ran and played for a bit until at last Molly, with Bounder beside her went up to the rabbit hutches to tell her story. But Maisy had a story of her own to tell!

As Vicky went to open the rabbit hutches, she yelled with glee as she discovered Maisy had given birth to five baby rabbits - three white ones, a brown one and a black one, all cuddled up in the straw beside her.

Dennis had known this would happen when he spoke to Rob in the park, though he didn't actually know it in his mind. He knew it through his intuition.

"Energy of thought travels a long, long way," Duncan said to Dennis and this time, Dennis heard a voice but wasn't sure whose voice it was, but he did know that energy indeed traveled a long, long way.

Daisy twitched her nose many times when she saw Molly, letting her know she was happy to have her friend back home again.

Duncan, now a father, as well as being the wisest rabbit of them all, kicked his hind legs five times on the back of his hutch, for we must not forget that Duncan was the father of these five babies. He had a family to look after now, and just then the clouds finally opened up and the rain came pouring down.

The End

ANIMAL SPIRIT INDEX

Frogs	Cleaning yourself from negativity
Dragonflies	Wisdom and communication
Fireflies	Bringing forth hope and light
Moths	Bringing money and abundance
Butterflies	Clarity and transformation
Squirrels	To find a safe place
Ant	Patience
Sparrows	Surviving and awakening, growth
Doves	Energy of peace and birth
Pigeons	Security
Budgerigar	Colours that bring about light energy
Woodpecker	Building your foundation
Cat	Mystery, magic and independence
Dog	Loyalty and looking for approval
Fox	Cunning, sly and having a disguise
Snake	Magic, change, wholeness
Spider	To create and to stop being so busy
Horse	Power
Bat	Rebirth...a fresh start
Badger	Bold self expression – keeper of stories
Dolphin	To be childlike
Skunk	Self respect - To like yourself
Porcupine	Play
Eagle	Freedom
Mouse	Caution...to be careful
Crow	Change, troubles...talk the truth
Rabbits	Stop to worry and stop being afraid
Racoon	Dexterity and disguise

John Fyfe is based in Montreal. Apart from being a writer he Is also a vedic astrologer, an explorer of the world where he has many wonderful friends. He also is a lover of animals.

John Fyfe learns to use an umbrella